# Mateship with Birds

Also by Carrie Tiffany

*Everyman's Rules for Scientific Living*

# Mateship
## with Birds

## CARRIE TIFFANY

PICADOR

First published 2012 in Picador by Pan Macmillan Australia Pty Limited, Sydney

First published in Great Britain 2012 by Picador
an imprint of Pan Macmillan, a division of Macmillan Publishers Limited
Pan Macmillan, 20 New Wharf Road, London N1 9RR
Basingstoke and Oxford
Associated companies throughout the world
www.panmacmillan.com

ISBN 978-1-4472-1986-6

1 3 5 7 9 8 6 4 2

A CIP catalogue record for this book is available from
the British Library.

Printed and bound by CPI Group (UK) Ltd, Croydon, CR0 4YY

*For Peter*

Birregurra, 1949: a boy of thirteen dies of tetanus after being pecked severely on the head by a magpie. Lake Boga, 1951: a local medical man nurses a magpie back to life after striking it with his car. When the bird duly recovers it returns to the bush bearing away the doctor's lower dentures. Cohuna, 1953: Trevor Mues is coasting up his driveway in his Ford utility when a magpie enters through the driver's side window, pecks him viciously on the ear and flies out through the window on the other side.

Kookaburras, magpies, butcherbirds, wagtails; the farm birds own the pasture and the bushes and the tree-top sky, but the parrots are supreme. The lemon-cresteds launch their scouts at sunrise, then the whole flock follows. In the few seconds before they rise the chiacking intensifies; as if each conversation must be shouted to conclusion before they are on the wing. Every morning the massed army of parrots – sometimes three or four hundred – fly inland to toil at the crops, every evening they return to the river to roost.

Harry watches the flock work the air as they leave. Their wing effort reduces as soon as they gain height and the sky opens up cleanly in front of them. It's dawn again. Milking again. The miracle of water into milk via grass must be performed at the start of each new day.

## COHUNA, 1953

Glenalpine Chrysanthemum, White-eye, Linga Longa
Wattle Flower, Banyule Tiddlewinks, Pineapple, Enid, Fatty,
Yarraview La Mode, Licker, Babs, Big Joyce, Wee Joyce,
Pauline, Stumbles and the others. They gather by the gate
in the half light, stamping their feet and swinging their hips
into the wind. He can see the outline of their faces through the
rain; their ears swivel towards him as he closes the back door.
He splashes through the puddles to the dairy, his head cocked
against the downpour. They watch him with the same deep
attention every day. As if they have just seen a new species for
the first time – a species that is not cow – and they mustn't
ever lose sight of it again. His milking clothes hang from a row
of horseshoes behind the bails: matted overalls stiff with mud
and faeces, a corrugated raincoat, a canvas apron florid with
milk mould. Pails and buckets from the wash room, hay spread

in each feeder, leg ropes kicked back and at the ready. He stands just under cover and looks out at the morning. There is more light now; he can see further across the paddocks. The rain is pooling badly in the low spots, if it doesn't let up soon the pasture will drown. He spits a mouthful of tobacco bile into the mud, pulls on the raincoat and goes out to fetch them. Sip is anxious to follow, but for the rain. She whimpers, hops from one front leg to the other, then slinks along the eaves, only darting out at the last minute, her ears flat against her neck.

On these wet mornings the world seems close around them – Harry and the herd. It is the same greasy rain that hits them both, that sticks to hide and skin, that gushes down their legs and gathers in their eyelashes. Harry opens the gate and pushes in among them. Their blood is hot. Each cow gives off her own great heat and takes in the heat of her sisters. They are urgent with milk and hunger, stamping and bellowing and thrusting out their necks. The damage is done here, when they are bagged-up and waiting – an udder squeezed against the fencepost, trodden on, torn or ripped. Harry flicks an old towel across their dented rumps, choosing who should go first and who should hang back. Sip lets off a few hoarse high-pitched barks from the sidelines. He has ten out now. They are docile into the bails, quick to get their heads down to the mash. The first cow brings back the feeling in his fingers. He slides his hands up and along the warm skin between her udder and her belly, throws up a mug of wash from the pail, sluices the whole thrumming organ, feels for the cups, tests the pull of suction and threads them on. Fat udders with bud teats, small, fruity udders with long spiked teats like landmines, slack udders, tight udders. Every day, twice a day, often with the help of young Michael from next door or Mues from over the road, Harry milks his herd.

Babs snorts pollard through her nostrils and swings her wet tail from side to side. Harry rinses her teats and pulls the cups off her. The rotary chuffs and swings overhead. They are slower to back out when it rains, hanging on for a few extra licks of the empty bucket, ignoring his voice and the flick of the towel, but when the balance tips and there are more out than in they start to hurry again. They don't fear Harry. They don't fear any man or dog, even a proper farm dog. What they fear is being alone. Being left behind. The last cow steps back. She looks in front of her at the long stream of cows ambling back to the paddock. She turns her wooden neck and looks behind her at the holding yard – empty. Her hooves scrape on the wet bricks. She bellows. Then she digs her back legs into the mud and runs out into the rain, her empty udder swinging slack and crumpled between her legs.

A whippet can't ride pillion on a motorcycle. Many farm dogs can; not a whippet. The whippet is too leggy, has no balance, insufficient courage and not enough fur. Harry takes his bike out for a weekly spin to clear the fluids and prevent the engine from getting stale. When he changes up to third the wind pulls at Sip's sparse coat. She leans hard against his chest for protection. She shivers violently, causing her bony bottom to lose traction with the saddle, causing her to tumble off sideways as they take the curve on Saleyards Road. Harry has never stopped faster. He nearly puts himself over the handlebars. He has to walk all of the way home with Sip hoisted over his shoulders. Mues isn't home so he asks Betty from next door to drive him back out to the bike and guide him home because the headlamp has blown and it's getting dark. The children want to come too, but Betty is firm with them. Michael has the dishes to dry and Little Hazel has her reader. Harry expects a bit of teasing; about the dog and the Waratah too.

'It's a constant labour of love,' Harry says as he gets out of the car and runs his hand over the leather saddle.

Betty looks at the motorcycle. The spray of red flowers painted on the petrol tank reminds her of a sewing machine, and there's Harry's birdwatching binoculars hanging from a special bracket he's welded onto the frame. There's nothing particularly masculine about it.

'It's just a constant labour, if you ask me,' Betty says. Then she turns the car around so he can ride in her lights on the way home.

She's an antler covered in warm velvet. Her legs are sticks; her yolky heart hangs in its brittle cage of ribs. She can't walk in a straight line. When Harry holds the gate open for her she slinks through it. She doesn't stand next to him like you might see a dog in a photograph, but with her back snaked around so it touches his leg. She's useless with the cows. She spends the winter curled up like a cat, she yelps at thunder, she's afraid of heights, she hates the rain. There's something obscene, dick-like, about the way her tail curves between her hind legs. She looks wounded when they go to town and he makes her jump down from the Dodge because he always lifts her when they are at home. Her whole existence, every sinewy fibre of her, is tuned to the feel of Harry's hand across the smooth cockpit of her skull.

The beloved have many names. Harry calls her sweetie, luvvie, goose and bag-o-bones. Mues calls her a dog-shaped-object or rat-on-stilts. He says, 'What's it shit like, Harry? Does it shit like a pencil?'

That first day when he collected her, and in the Dodge on the way home took off his coat and tucked it around her shoulders … it went along the usual way after that. An alteration in the focal length – each fixed for the gaze of the other. The imbibing of odours. The warm soil of her head, the bread and vinegar of his crotch. A babble language followed quickly by regret for the first hard words. Physical changes. The sharing of personality and mannerisms.

All her expressions are known to him. Her squinted blink, the thwop of ropey tail against the lino, the shame-clamped jaw. Then familiarity. Indifference. Forgetfully, he sometimes runs his hand across her ribs. If it's early on in the week, a Monday or a Tuesday, he'll say, 'That's enough then. That'll do you for the rest of the week,' and she'll lean into his knees, blissful at the sound of his voice.

Little Hazel walks to the Leitchville Road to catch the school bus into Cohuna. Her shoes scuff through the dirt. She carries her metal school tin with a date scone rolling around inside it. The sun is already high and strong in the sky behind her. She turns out of the driveway and into the road. The air smells warm and wet and faintly ripe like fruit just on the turn – a mixture of sun-baked cow shit and algae ripening in the irrigation channels of the dairy farm next door. She looks warily at a row of magpies on the wire fence. They aren't looking at her, but it is nearly swooping season so she puts her school tin on her head just in case. She can see Mr Mues leaning on his gate up ahead. Her arm is getting tired holding the tin in place so she tries to balance it for a few steps like an African, but it drops and she bends over to pick it up from the dirt.

'Michael not going to school today?' Mues calls out to her.

'Nope. He's sick.'

'How's he sick then?' Mues has a pouchy face and red-rimmed eyes with too much of the inner lid, the inner workings, on display.

'He's got the runs.'

Mues nods sympathetically.

Little Hazel walks on and is almost out of earshot when he calls out to her again.

'Do you want to come in for a minute and see my pony?'

She stops and considers. Mues's place is a mess of rusty old machinery and kennels and laundries and packing sheds. She's never seen a pony, but perhaps he keeps it inside, or perhaps it's new? She hears him sniff behind her and the sound of the chain jiggling on the gatepost.

'It's a Shetland pony.'

She follows him into a rundown shed – dim and thick with flies. She keeps her distance from him. He's busy with something in the corner. She thinks he is shielding the pony from her to make it more of a surprise. It must, she thinks, be very tiny, probably just a foal. She is trying to look around him, into the corner, when he turns, his trousers slide slowly down his legs, the end of his belt curves around his ankles like a tail and she sees that he is not wearing underpants. That he is holding his shirt up on purpose to reveal his dick, all raw and swollen pink. It is hoisting itself up with wobbly effort like a mechanical toy. Little Hazel frowns, tries again to look behind him for the pony, then returns her gaze to the dick. She looks at the spot on the roof that the dick is pointing to. There are a few cobwebs draped between the rafters and several small shafts of light beaming through the holes in the rusty iron. Little Hazel doesn't scream, doesn't feel sick, doesn't run away. She just feels disappointed. Hugely disappointed. She thinks that it has all been pointless – the cutting-out of pictures from magazines, the books borrowed from the library. The drawings attempted, rubbed out, attempted again in her treasured scrapbook where the Shetland's neck was always too long or the Shetland's legs too thin, or she'd had to use blue for the tail as the black had run out. At that moment Little Hazel understands that she will never, ever, get a Shetland pony. Her life will be no different to everybody else's – made up of cobbling things together that are misshapen, ill-suited, imperfect. That wanting something badly is not enough to get it. And adults are part of this pretence – they hold one thing in their hand and call it another. Hazel picks up her school tin and leaves. She isn't even late for the bus.

Betty tries not to look at her reflection in the co-op window. She glances. There's nobody about. She stands in front of the glass, pulls her stomach in and smiles. The puffy flesh of her cheeks rises up around her eyes and she is brought up sharp by the sight of herself so doughy, so exposed, like when her hair has just been cut and set and there is too much of herself on display. This is how she feels most of the time now; always blowzy, always overstuffed. She can't stop touching the flesh that rolls over the waistband of her skirt, or fingering the mounds that form on either side of her bra straps. She looks at her legs as she peels off her stockings in the evenings; everything is dragging downwards – the heaviness of her thighs has settled lower around her knees and calves; the bones of her ankles are going under. She tells herself there's nothing to worry about when she's out in public, when she's dressed, with lipstick. But here, standing in the main street, in front of the glass … She looks at herself side on, sees her ear and her head above it where patches of dry white scalp show through between the curls of her permanent. The curls don't look like hair; they look like something made out of hair that has been stored in the back of a cupboard. She moves closer to the glass, examines the deep grooves in the skin around her mouth where it meets the deflated flesh of her lips. The lines around her mouth and the scored skin between her eyes – a fork mark – make her look angry and tired; tired in a way that sleep can't fix. Her finger is on her lip, in that private place underneath the nostrils.

'Morning.'

Betty reaches out and steadies herself against the glass.

'You right there?'

She turns around. Harry removes the pipe from his mouth with one hand and puts it back again with the other.

'Trying to remember my list, and that.'

He nods, takes a few puffs on his unlit pipe and stands awkwardly. Betty looks down at his boots. Harry kicks up one leg and knocks his pipe out against the raised heel. They both look up again. Harry coughs.

'Been hot.'

'Hotter last week though.'

'True.'

Betty lifts her hand and pats a curl against her neck. Harry looks off down the street, looks back at her, coughs again.

'I've mice in the shed – can you get Michael to bring Louie over?'

Betty nods and smiles. Harry touches his hat and walks away. She parts the fly strips at the co-op door and takes a basket from the stack.

For God's sake, she says to herself, for God's sake, woman, who do you think you are?


Who does she think she is? Betty Reynolds is a woman of forty-five, is the mother of Little Hazel and Michael, is an aide at the Acacia Court Home for the Aged. She rents a small house on the outskirts of Cohuna next to a dairy farm. She drives a Vauxhall. She came here pregnant with Little Hazel, Michael still in short pants by her side. The people of Cohuna assume that she must have had, at some stage, a husband – perhaps killed in the war? Apart from her work and her children Betty keeps to herself. She wears no rings. She doesn't correct people when they call her Mrs Reynolds, but she refers to herself as just Betty or, where possible, Michael and Hazel's mum. And there are times when this seems remarkable to her – that she is so convincingly in the present – that she carries no mark, or gives off no hint, of the difficulties of her past.

The people of Cohuna have not seen Betty Reynolds hopeful as she dabs on her lipstick in the morning and then resigned as she wipes it off at night. They have not seen the pile of lipstick-stained tissues that grows day after day in the cheap cane rubbish bin under her dresser to be emptied on Saturday and used to light the fire. They have not seen her undressing in front of the wardrobe mirror, slowly removing her slip, cupping her large, pale breasts in her hands, plucking the hairs that have started to grow around the nipples. They have not seen her grimacing at the exquisite sting of the tweezers, then having to soothe the skin with cold cream and finding herself overcome. Finding herself standing in front of the mirror scolding and hating herself and wondering who she is hurting herself for, and why her body is turning into something else before she has had a chance to discover what it was before. And then getting into bed with scenes replaying in her head from so long ago she is no longer sure if they are memory or fantasy. She cries often, in her bed, and when the tears subside begins to feel the heat and weight of herself keenly against the mattress. She rolls onto her back and wipes her hands across her breasts. She brings her palms to her face and breathes in the mix of sweat and glycerin. Her fingers separate the sticky curls of her bush. It is never the same. Some nights it is all she can do to stroke herself slowly up and over the wave. Other nights she thrashes, climbs steeply, stops, spits on her fingers, starts again and has to beg someone – someone who isn't there – before she can reach release.

By daybreak her bladder is aching and she gets up to piss. Around four each morning she pads down the path to the outhouse and takes the temperature of the day ahead. Sometimes the winking owl is perched on the post of the washing line. Its bulging eyes and flattened face seem mongoloid – both innocent and evil. The beak is worn; stained and twisted like the dew claw on an old dog. They look at each other seriously. The owl is gone when she returns. She never sees it on the wing.

And then, just after dawn, nobody sees Betty Reynolds as she dresses and sets the fire and makes the tea. As she calls out for Michael and Little Hazel and stands at the window pulling her cardigan tight, looking out at the frost on the pasture and getting on with the day for there is nothing else to be done with it.

Betty can hardly remember back to the time when Harry was a stranger to them. But he rarely came to the house when they first arrived. It was more usual for them to meet in town. Harry offered to hold baby Hazel while Betty got a prescription filled at the chemist. When she returned they sat together on the bench outside the post office. A crow called lazily from the top of the water tower. It was warming up and still early in the day. Betty remembers the condensed blue of the sky – she wasn't used to it then, the tinted Cohuna sky.

'Are you going to give her back then?'

Harry looked down at the sleeping baby. A circle of milk-flecked saliva cooled on the inside of his arm. 'Yes, of course.' He handed her back to Betty. 'Very nice, babies – aren't they?'

'Much like adults really, only smaller.'

'That's right.' Harry perked up. 'Much like regular folk, only a different shape. It's the shape that confuses – and there's so much wrapping you never know which end you're talking to.'

Betty cuffed him across the shoulder and stood up to leave. She smiled. He smiled back.

Even after that Harry was hesitant about coming inside Betty's house. He'd hold the fly-wire door open and stand stiffly in the doorframe – a portrait of a man unsure of his welcome. Or he'd stay out on the verandah.

Michael reads to Betty as she peels potatoes in the sink. The white flesh turns around and around under the knife in her hand. Michael rocks on his chair at the kitchen table, shadowing the lines in *Science for Young Australians* with his finger. Harry listens from the verandah.

'The Laughing Kookaburra, or Laughing Jack, or Alarmbird, or Breakfastbird, or Shepherd's Clock, or Woop Woop Pigeon is a boisterous bird of the Australian bush known for its raucous laugh.' Michael stumbles on 'raucous'. Betty corrects him.

'Raw-cous,' he says. 'Laughing Jack spends his days hunting throughout this territory and comes home of an evening to lead the family chor-us. These birds, from the kingfisher family, have an unusual family structure. Groups of adult males and females live in celibacy with one central couple and assist them in hunting and raising their young.' Michael's finger has halted under 'celibacy' – he looks up at his mother.

'Go on, Michael, love,' Betty says, her voice high and formal. She turns back to the sink, her curls joggle against her neck as she reaches for another potato.

Harry knows all this, of course; he knows everything about birds.

After a few years they have the impression that Harry is always there, but in fact he is only ever there in small snatches – a meal, the delivery of a particular item, collecting Michael to help with the cows. The operations of the family are attractive to him, but also unsettling. When he's invited to tea he leaves immediately the meal is finished, as if unsure of what happens next.

The year that Little Hazel turns eight Harry helps her make a present for her mother – a pokerwork sign for the house. They work in the dairy. The girl's hands wrapped in rags to protect them from the hot poker; Harry taking over when she loses interest and finishing it off with a chisel to give it a decorative edge. Harry says it is all her work, although she knows it isn't.

On Christmas Day Little Hazel goes to collect Harry. She wears a green skating dress with ten large white buttons down the front. It looks odd; like a uniform. She saw the pattern in *Woman's Day* and wouldn't let up until Betty made it for her. She has her scuffed leather school shoes on and no socks. Harry wears a cream shirt, braces and his good trousers. His beard is freshly trimmed. Harry notices that the girl is walking strangely. At each step she kicks her knees up and watches as the green skirt flicks around her legs. It's a worrying age for a girl child, Harry thinks. An age when they can start to impersonate themselves.

After the Christmas dinner shared with Sip and the Christmas pudding with a saucer of cream for Louie, Harry mounts the sign on the weatherboards next to the front door. It's twilight, the air is full of summer insects. They stand back to admire the sign. Little Hazel gives it a once-over with the hem of her dress. REYNOLDS it says, not quite centred on a slab of red gum. The sound of the cicadas is amplified as the light fades. Betty turns around. Harry has gone. She can see a dark shape moving behind the sugar gums and just in front of it the orange glow of his pipe that looks to be leading him away.

The pull between the boy and the man is much like that between the man and the dog. Soon Michael is at Harry's most afternoons after school, and on the weekends they go fishing together or rabbiting. Betty walks out of the kitchen, a basin on her hip, to see them sitting on the step together with one of Harry's bird books and the binoculars. She overhears Harry's directions to Michael; gentle, low-voiced, almost swallowed in his beard. 'Fantail at four o'clock.' There's a way they have of half turning their faces towards each other. Betty is tipping the sink water on the tomatoes when Michael calls out to her for assistance. He's trying to tie a handkerchief over Harry's eyes so he can record how many birds Harry can identify in five minutes by call alone.

Betty kneels down and pulls the material taut across Harry's thinning hair. Then she holds his head in her hands and turns it from side to side to check his ears aren't impeded.

'Can I start now?' Harry asks Michael.

Michael checks Harry's wristwatch.

'Ten seconds.' Michael counts the seconds down by tapping his finger on his leg. Betty notices the length of Michael's thighs; how quickly he is growing. She stands up and smooths down her skirt.

'Directly behind us, Michael,' Harry says. 'Number one: a Mother Bird.'

One evening, Harry edges carefully up the track and parks at the edge of the channel. He rubs his palms on the steering wheel. 'We can walk along here a bit. I need to check the water, see how she's flowing.'

Betty looks across at him and smiles. She likes to sit in Harry's Dodge. The seat is low and sleek like an upholstered banquette at a fancy restaurant and it smells of hay and boot polish. She looks out of the windscreen at the scene framed in front of her. The channel has an oasis quality. Water seeps through the channel banks to the weeds and wildflowers, marking out a strip of bright green from the grey of the paddocks. At either side of the car large river red gums are anchored to the bank just as a painter would place them at the outer edges of a canvas for balance and perspective. Harry takes his foot off the brake and the car settles under them.

'Alright then?'

Betty nods. 'Alright then.'

They walk for a while along the edge of the bank, Harry stopping now and then to measure the channel depth and test the flow of water around his outstretched fingers. The hot edge has gone off the afternoon. There doesn't seem much need for talk. The bank is narrow so they walk slowly, in single file. Betty is in the lead; Harry hangs far enough back so he can watch the way she moves. He likes her plump forearms, the cardigan pushed up around them; the gilt band of her watch digging into her wrist. He likes the sound of her clothes moving around her middle. When she turns to speak to him he notices her softening jaw and her mouth – the lipstick on her front teeth. He's been watching all of this, over the years, watching her body age and temper.

They reach the fence and turn back again towards the car. Harry scans the bank for a flat section with decent grass. He points it out to her. 'Sit down there a bit and take your shoes off.'

'Give my bunions a breather?'

'I didn't know you had bunions. That's a bonus.' He takes his coat off and lays it down for her. They sit for a while, murmuring the odd comment into the afternoon; watching the birds flit between the trees and the water.

Betty needs to get tea on, and there's work tomorrow. The day is closing in. He follows her back to the car. The grass has made an intricate scribbled pattern on the backs of her legs. It reminds Harry of ancient Egyptian writing he's seen in books; hieroglyphics. He wonders if the scholars are mistaken, if hieroglyphics is not a written language after all, but the marks early crops made on the skin of women when they lay down in the fields to rest.

Harry makes the grass brand from a stirrup iron. He solders the plate of patterned tin over the opening where the ball of the foot sits. Two harness traces form a handle. It has taken many hours of work with the tin cutters to match the whorls and intersections in the tin with his memory of the grass pattern on Betty's legs. Countless times, in the making, he has wiped the tin on a rag and tried it on his own leg.

Sunday evening, Harry wraps the brand in a clean tea towel and walks over to Betty's. He's always expected for tea on a Sunday. He has his good jacket on, but his shirt cuffs are still rolled thickly at the elbow so it isn't sitting right. He's not sure what he's going to say to Betty about the brand. He's hoping explanations won't be necessary – that she'll just take it, that she'll understand.

Dora from the poultry farm is sitting in Harry's place at the kitchen table. She's sipping lemon cordial and leaving her orange lipstick on the rim of the glass. A chair is brought in for Harry and he sits at the corner of the table straddling one of its legs. Little Hazel passes Harry the gravy, but she can't take her eyes off Dora. Betty explains that Dora and Michael are working on a project together for school. Michael mumbles in agreement, a crop of pimples reddening around his nose. Betty returns to her dinner, forking her peas with care. Harry feels uneasy listening to Dora and Michael talk – as if he's eavesdropping on something encoded and private. Four is comfortable, everyone has their place; five feels lopsided, unbalanced somehow. After dinner Michael and Dora go into the front room to listen to the wireless. Dora is interested in next year's royal tour. She's brought her scrapbook in case anything new is mentioned. Betty washes the dishes, Little Hazel dries. Harry sits at the table behind them with his cup of tea cooling in front of him. Little Hazel places the clean plates, the baking dishes, the egg-beater and the slotted spoon on the table. This is the time, after dinner, that Michael would usually get his bird books out and they'd chat about the week's sightings. The brand is still on Harry's lap. He considers unwrapping it and putting it on the table with the kitchen utensils, it wouldn't look out of place – or not immediately so. He says goodnight to Betty and Little Hazel and scratches Louie under the chin. He calls out to Michael in the sitting room, there is no reply. On the way home Harry stops at the dairy. He hangs the brand from a rusty nail on the wall. As time goes by it looks more and more like an implement that every dairy farmer would have.

On the shelf in the dairy: Provet Vaginitis Powder; Ammolene Dairy Cleanser; Hamilton Mammitis Vaccine; Provet Teat Salve; Provet Blighty; Killaweed; Sykes's Bag Balm – keeps teats as soft as silk; Immunol Organic Lime Compound; various discarded medicated licks – they didn't work, but he can't quite bring himself to throw them out; Calcijec for milk fever and grass tetany; Fumoflake calcium cyanide for gassing rabbit burrows; a copy of *The Right Way!* by John Roy Stewart, a veterinary book on how to treat the disease and how to perform the operation; numerous unread reports of milk, butter and cream equalisation and stabilisation schemes; and a flyer promoting a screening of Egg Petersen's colour film, *No Hand Stripping*, held at the Cohuna Mechanics Institute four years ago.

The forecast says some stratocumulus moving over at times from the north, but it should fine up nicely later on, it should give Harry a clear run at fixing the fence in the channel paddock. He starts the vacuum pump on the milking machine, rinses the glass observation bowl and tensions the inflations. The first cows trot forwards into the bails. Licker and Big Joyce are jostling for their place in line. Harry hears their hooves skittering on the bricks. He looks up from taking the cups off Stumbles to see Licker with her head down shoving Big Joyce out of the way. Licker often has a large mood on her. The top cows and the bottom cows are not the problem – it's the middle classes that are always jockeying for position, trying to better themselves and knocking each other about in the process. Harry is careful not to pet a middle cow – even the smallest attention and she'll be high-hatting her sisters and become even more unmanageable. Joyce takes the shove at the worst place – just below the hips where she's not very stable, where the weight of her udder is already pulling her off-balance. Her knees splay out from under her; she teeters pathetically on the edges of her hooves. Licker trots smartly through the gap and shoves her head into the trough to feed.

'Really, girls,' Harry says. 'Is that really necessary?'

He moves smoothly between each cow, going backwards and forwards into the engine room, checking the separator. When the rhythm of the milking is well underway he lets his mind wander. Harry entertains himself with the idea that the girls are a troupe – perhaps dancers or singers – and that he is their manager, responsible for their myriad complex travel arrangements and costumes and meals. They are on some sort of vague world tour where they are much acclaimed for their talent and beauty. Harry is a dedicated but exasperated manager, worn down by attending to all of their feminine needs and foibles. He's responsible too for their reputations. When Babs leaves the stalls at unexplained speed, her empty udder slapping slackly between her legs, he watches after her and feels ashamed on her behalf, hoping nobody has seen his good girl with her bloomers showing. Harry shakes his head and finishes rinsing the udder in his hands the tight bag of a milker in her first lactation. Four cows to go now. The pump is chugging along warmly. Harry wonders what grand city they are in today. He sees bold headlines in foreign newspapers, imagines them being met in the foyers of expensive hotels. The sound of their breathing falls into line with the pulse of the cups inflating. Harry is their conductor – he's at the centre of an orchestra of pistons, lungs and udders. The cows provide the wheezy melody, the milking machine bashes along underneath with its regular motorised beat. It's Harry's music-de-milk and the dawn is only just breaking.

As he washes the buckets out Harry sees Tiny admiring her reflection in the wing mirror of the Waratah. She sits perched on the handlebars turning her head from side to side in front of the glossy circle. Tiny is the smallest, most dim-witted member of the family of kookaburras that live on Harry's farm. Nearly all well-run dairy farms with their irrigation channels and fertile pastures, their thick shelterbelts to protect the cows from wind and rain, can attract enough insects, lizards, frogs and small birds to support a kookaburra family. Harry and Michael keep a weather eye on the kookaburras. They are brash and rowdy, more like dogs than birds. Tiny hammers her beak into the mirror. The force of it knocks the bike from its stand and it clatters to the ground. Tiny, startled, flies away so hurriedly one of her wings clips the gatepost and she veers clumsily towards the mud. Harry shakes his head at her in exasperation, but he's smiling as he rights the bike and checks it for damage. It's something to be shared with Michael, although Harry is not sure Michael will be interested while young Dora is on the scene. Harry takes an old milk ledger from the bottom shelf in the dairy. The left-hand column is full of pencilled figures, but the right-hand column is blank throughout the book. It's wide enough for a few notes, and it's better than leaving the paper unused or buying a new book. Harry writes, '*Observations of a Kookaburra Family at Cohuna*', and underlines it twice. He's not sure about the pitch of it, or how to begin. So he imagines he's talking birds with Michael, licks his pencil and starts to write.

The day starts in their throats.
Dad first, then Mum,
Tiny and Club-Toe.
The four of them in the red gum
by the dairy.
As regular as clockwork
they make their request for air.

Most afternoons
Mum and Dad nap in the old angophora.
The aunts take off –
flying the boundaries,
hunting,
spying on the neighbours.
But for several hours Mum and Dad
share a perch,
and do nothing at all.
They sit very still,
a couple of woody fruits
budded to the branch.

Jewel beetles,
longicorn beetles,
stag beetles,
chafers,

earwigs,
weevils,
spider – one leg only,
lizard – one almost complete,
bones of three others,
two mice mandibles,
six (v. large mouse or rat?) mandibles,
a long aquatic feeler – catfish, maybe a yabbie?
Three complete beaks,
one partial beak.
All of this in a handful of pellets
under the roost tree.
I sliced them open with my knife.
There's a high percentage of waste,
but a beak isn't like a mouth.
There's no tongue for tasting.
Just some sort of mechanism
that decides what goes down,
and what comes up.

A spot of family boxing after the rain blows over.
Mum is challenged by Club-Toe.
She's all bluster;
a bit of wing action,
some bobbing up and down on the branch,

a few jabs with her beak.
Mum stands her ground,
doesn't move, doesn't blink,
just turns her head towards the offensive.
After a while Club-Toe cracks the sulks
and flies off to a distant tree.
She's back by teatime,
taking her place in the chorus,
singing her familiar lines.

Their primary address
is a large red gum by the dairy.
But they also reside
in your mum's peppercorn,
in the bundy box in Mues's front garden,
in the old angophora behind the channel,
in the sugar gums that line the driveway
and the road.

Mum and Dad I understand –
your typical marital pair.
But why do the ladies stay on?
Club-Toe and Tiny
are fully grown,
are fit enough to feed themselves.

They slope off during the day,
stray towards the boundaries,
do some show-off flying
where the neighbours can see.
Yet each dusk and dawn
they are back in the family chorus,
right on song.

When Mues was here the other day
he threw his cigarette butt away – still lit, of course.
Mum was watching us
from the roof of the tractor shed.
She flew down
and picked the butt up in her beak.
I had the cows in so I couldn't follow her,
but she took it back to the roost tree, I'm sure of it,
for what –
a family smoke bath –
a delousing of the lot of them?

A high branch is chosen for hunting.
The kookaburra sits,
watching the ground,
waiting for something to move across its eye.
Then it drops through all that air;

silent, lead-beaked,
like an anchor through seawater.


Dad isn't large, but he's pretty;
the mask of dark feathers across his eyes,
the flash of blue on his rump.
A bandit-dandy.
He flies the boundaries in the mornings,
keeps the airy fences in place.
Then it's preening and snacking
until the evening concert,
when he sounds the first note.
I get the sense that if he wasn't there,
they wouldn't sing at all.


Watching Tiny in the peppercorn
during the day.
She sits for hours,
motionless,
her beak splayed open,
waiting for something to pass across her eye.
She's a vacant lot, that bird;
gormless,
I worry for her future.

Wing boxing,
sparring,
beak locking,
beak twisting and grasping
until one bird flies away,
or is knocked from the perch,
is constant throughout the year.

There's a small family
across the road at Mues's;
three birds only.
And to the west
a large noisy mob;
six at least.

When the air is dry and thin
(early February),
you can hear the river birds to the north.
I thought at first
they were an echo,
but when you get your ear in
it's clear
that each family sings its own song.

Betty keeps a notebook in her handbag with a record of the children's illnesses and accidents. When she arrives home in the evening after work and hears their voices, bored and ordinary in the kitchen, she feels a rush of relief. The children are safe. Another day has passed and she has not failed to keep them safe.

### 1945/46

**Michael:** Burns hair at stove, pecked by gander, warts, skewered with fork, constipation, infected splinters, ball-bearing lodged in ear, sticky eye, fevers, boils

**Little Hazel:** Colic, croup, nappy rash, fever, runny stools, earache.

### 1947/48

**Michael:** Stood on by sheep, wasp stings, chickenpox, swallowed petrol, nits, carbuncles, trampled by cow, pecked on eyelid by bird, tonsillitis, constipation, warts, chilblains, swallowed coin.

**Little Hazel:** Croup, chickenpox, tummy upset, scalds hand on teapot, hives.

At five Michael steals a penny from Betty's purse. Not to spend – he likes the feel of the coin in his pocket, likes to run his fingers over the big buck kangaroo. Betty doesn't have the heart to pull his pants down so she smacks him with the wooden spoon through his shorts and shirt-tails and underpants so she isn't really hitting him at all, just whacking at the layers of clothing and the air trapped between them. He's never been smacked before. As soon as she releases him he turns on her. He looks about the kitchen in fury and waves his small fist at her. 'How dare you? You pan, you rug, you – you – you … *spoon.*'

She gasps. She covers her face with her hands. He's right, she isn't a bitch or a slut; she is a pan, a rug, a spoon. She is a woman without a man – a utensil inside a house.

1949/50

**Michael:** Bitten by bull ants, fish hook stuck in thumb, infected scratch from goanna, constipation, fever, bronchitis, warts, boils, chilblains, corns.

**Little Hazel:** German measles, carbuncles, sticky eyes, chilblains, wandering off.

At three and a half Little Hazel gets a lift into town on the milk truck not wearing her underpants. Betty is in the co-op buying bacon when Mervyn Plimeroll brings her in. Mervyn tells Betty he found her sitting on the road sniffling and asking to be taken to the lolly shops. Mervyn looks embarrassed. He's holding the little girl's hand, but standing as far away from her as possible. He transfers the small hot hand to Betty. Betty apologises and thanks him. She shakes her head at Little Hazel and lines up for the cash register. Little Hazel is tired. She picks up the hem of her cotton smock and puts it in her mouth to suck. There are her legs, the strong thighs swagged with baby fat. And there, between her legs, is her plump white purse. The slit is a mere smudge and wouldn't draw the eye, but for the lips which are the same pink – the same pure, baby's pink – as the lips of her rosy mouth.

1951/52

**Michael:** Concussion from bicycle accident, infected toe from spider bite (?), kicked by cow, v. bad cough, pecked by gander, eye infection, warts on feet, skewered with fork, burnt foot, constipation, infected splinters, nits.

**Little Hazel:** Tummy upset, headaches, chilblains, pecked by gander, warts, cough, scratched by cat, diarrhoea, nits.

Michael asks Betty about his father just as he is starting school. He has been plaguing her with questions – what is our last name, do we have a nice house, will my shorts be the same as the other boys' shorts? Betty gets him a kitten. Within a year the cat has her own kittens and is immediately sick of the sight of them. She takes off into the paddocks for days, returning to slump down exhausted on one of the kittens, crushing its eye into the socket. Betty and Michael keep the injured kitten in a biscuit tin and watch as its recessed eye turns chalky and dies. Michael doesn't want to look at the kitten then, he tries to close the lid on it, but Betty holds his hand and makes him stroke its back. When Michael is asleep Betty takes the kitten and wraps it in a tea towel with its tiny head exposed. She grips the bundle between her knees and sews the kitten's eyelid closed with thread. She sews at the kitchen table, under the electric light, with the sound of the wind rattling the back door in its frame. In the morning Michael slips into his mother's bed with the one-eyed kitten in the pocket of his dressing gown. This is the one they keep. Louie. Black and white Louie with cobwebs in her whiskers. Louie the mouser. Just like her mother Louie goes off into the paddocks for days and they love her even more when she comes home.

1953

**Michael:** Constipation, cough, infected hand, wasp sting, skin troubles, cut foot with axe, concussion in fall from railway bridge, boys' troubles.

**Little Hazel:** Bitten by Foot Foot, school cough, rashes, bruises from Foot Foot, tonsillitis, boils, nits, warts on hands.

Driving in to work at Acacia Court, Betty often sees two little boys playing on a billycart in front of their house – the newsagent's twins. She waves and looks back at them in her rear-vision mirror as they drag bits of wood and tin across the gutter to make ramps and bridges. Their padded faces are flushed with effort and concentration. The boys are so busy they barely notice the passing car. And they are too young to recognise the routine – that Betty passes at this same time every day of the working week.

She can see the car park from all of the windows in Lilac ward and from the kitchen and the office. There are three crows on the edge of the incinerator and another on the rail of the mortuary ramp. The night girl has written '*all quite*' in the record book. It is not easy to hold the checks of Bert's arse apart – the muscles have slackened like spent tyre tubes. She looks out of the window. A crow hops onto the bonnet of her car with a piece of rubbish in its beak. Bert has a faecal impaction; a hard mass of faeces in the rectum is obstructing the neck of his bladder. Lately, small amounts of liquid faeces have leaked around the bolus, giving the false impression of diarrhoea. Remove the bolus, restore continence. Bert's shit has the consistency of tar. She edges her finger between the mass and the bowel wall. It's the same technique as getting a burnt cake out of a tin. She extracts her finger and keeping her gloved hands well up in the air takes two steps to the window and hits it with her elbow to shoo the crow away. 'Hang on, sweetie,' she says to Bert. 'I'll be back with some Vaseline.'

Stan Ebersole, Reg Healy, Ern Lillee, Dennis Popp, Harold Carton, Mervyn Whipp, Bert Plimeroll, Magnus, Pinky Giddings, Bill Sickle, Jack McGordon, Donald Arbuthnot, Cliff Heaslip, Arthur Springgay. They have the new linoleum, easy-clean and as cool as glass. They have the Brumly geriatric chair, non-tippable and posturally appropriate. They have a round table to play cards at and plastic spout cups to drink from. Betty has her favourites in the same way a mother has a favourite child. Cliff with his poet's face, Jack's hands – she imagines them on her sometimes as she cleans his nails. Ern has something, in his confusion. Bill who came in with blue marks all over his body – his wife never gave up sleeping next to him, despite his incontinence. For three years she wore her blue plastic raincoat to bed each night and then she died.

Mervyn says, 'At night I hear the train coming. It says, home, home, home. But it isn't stopping anywhere near here and there's nobody on it for me.'

Reg says, 'I saw an ant on my cupboard and I put some biscuit there, so it makes it through the winter.'

Stan says, 'A proper cup. Don't put that dick spout in my mouth.'

Ern says, 'Sat around bubba then but tits tea go poor mopey it boil bud shilling vanished she's what sore brown it fence was billy pecked.' Because he's had three strokes and along the way his words have come uncoupled from their meaning.

Cliff says, 'I'm as mad as a wet bee.'

Betty moves from station to station wiping each bedside cabinet. She removes the water glass and fills it; rinses and replaces the expectoration mug. She disposes of hidden food, straightens the racing guide, removes lumps of ear wax smeared on bed rails and closes the matchbox where Des Feely has his collection of chewed-off fingernails. She works around the precious things – a handkerchief with a pet name, a well-fingered lingerie advertisement, a German coin. Cliff has a notebook for his memoirs – most of the pages are blank but a few feature the same drawing of an erect cock and balls shooting semen straight out like bullets from a gun.

A ten-year-old boy would draw this on a toilet wall. Whose fault is it that their bodies are crumbling when their feelings are still ripe?

There are three women in the day room looking at the linoleum. It's the new no-wax in high-sheen apple green. The purchase and installation of the linoleum was written up in the local paper and now several times a week a group of women drop by to see it. A carload of friends or neighbours from Deniliquin, Echuca, Kerang or Swan Hill make a day of it with sandwiches and a thermos. Betty hears them say, 'You could eat your dinner off it,' or, 'It's like silk, like liquid silk.' Most of them think they see a fault over by the windows, but it is just the reflection of the oleander in the glass. Betty pushes Stan through the double doors in his wheelchair with one hand and leads Reg by the elbow with the other. Two of the women see Betty enter and move politely back against the wall. The third woman, younger with a thick waist and poodle curls, has taken off her shoes and is scooting about in her stockinged feet pretending that she's skiing. Betty comes up soundlessly behind her and the young woman startles, her feet slide out from under her and she nearly falls into Stan's lap. 'Slippery, huh?' she says with a gasp. Her curls bobble frantically around her head as she regains her balance. Her friends start to giggle and Stan laughs too. He says, 'Slippery, huh? Slippery, huh?'over and over again. Betty has draped a blanket across his lap so the women don't see that his hands are deep inside his pyjama trousers doing what they're always doing – working away at his limp old cock. Stan has nothing to say about floor coverings.

Dressing, toileting, feeding, toileting, milky drinks, mashed vegetables, jelly, toileting. The birthday day – to make it easier they share a birthday, like horses, and a yellow cake. She thinks they might as well all be leading the same life.

In her lunch hour Betty goes to her locker and gets her hat and bag. She puts on some lipstick and a spray of Tweed. She leaves through the back door and comes in again through the front. It started with Bill – no living relatives – but now it has grown to include all of the widowers. She draws the visitor's chair up to Jack's bed and reaches out for his hand on the blanket. She notices the clock on the wall ticks loudly for a few seconds and then quiets down. Jack blinks at her and she smiles proudly at him, coaxing him to respond. Why shouldn't I get to be a wife? Betty thinks. Why shouldn't I get to be a wife to them all?

Jack pushes himself up on his elbows. He says, 'You can kill me when I no longer enjoy a cup of tea.'

Behind the last of Mues's out sheds, in between the woodpile and the paddock where he keeps his killers, is the rusty shell of his dad's first Ford. The tray and the back axle were cut off years ago for some other agricultural purpose, the windscreen's shot, the doors and wheels are long gone, but the seat is still serviceable and sometimes Mues slides in behind the big dinner plate steering wheel to cogitate and smoke a pipe. This late afternoon a couple of sulphur-crested cockatoos are cleaning up around the fence line in front of him. There's a big old male and his missus strutting and bobbing – passing bits of straw from claw to beak. Mues watches them for a while then tiptoes to the house for his shotgun. The birds are still there when he returns. He slips back into the car seat and rests the barrel of the gun on the dashboard. He waits for the male to appear from behind a fencepost, raises the gun and shoots. The air around the bird is hazed briefly with a cloud of white belly feathers. The other bird, the female, lifts quickly in panic and flies off towards the creek, her wing beats sounding strong and urgent like a tarp being shaken in the wind.

Mues taps his pipe out on the chassis and fills it again. He pushes his thumb under the surface rust where the running board curves up into the mudguard and watches it flake off. After a few minutes the female bird returns. She lands close to the body of the male and uses her beak to lift his limp head up from the ground. She does this again and again. Then she leaves his head and climbs unsteadily up onto his body – walking to and fro down his length, holding on, gripping and squeezing him with her claws. She flies away and Mues thinks it is all over, but after a few minutes she returns. This time she has a few stems of wallaby grass in her beak. She lays the grass down next to the body of the male and goes back to scratching along the fence line. After a few bobs and scratches she stops and watches him. When she sees that he doesn't eat, she returns to his body and tries again to lift his head from the ground and to trample on him. There's something both comical and grotesque about her – her fanning headgear, the leering half-moon curve of her beak. Mues is reminded of a Punch and Judy show he saw at the Echuca agricultural show as a boy. Of sitting between his mother and father in this same seat for the long drive, of his hand sweating against his mother's leg. The beaky puppets fought and jeered and hit each other with sticks, their lips a glossy, painful red. There was a string of tiny sausages made from women's stockings. He remembers that he wanted to touch them.

It is starting to get dark. Mues shifts his weight on the seat. He reaches down for the gun, the barrel is still pleasantly warm in his hands. He takes the gun to his shoulder and shoots the remaining bird.

Dairy pastures are difficult to establish in gullies where there is seepage and drainage. They drift like continents; their hides are maps of uncharted countries. Keep the herd on dry ground through the winter. Sunlight shines ginger through their ears. Plant shelterbelts to reduce wind speed. Elastic ropes of snot hang from their nostrils; their hocks are stuck with shit.

Harry checks the herd for wooden tongue and eats his lunch leaning against the fence. Corned beef and tomato sauce, a thick coating of dripping to counteract the age of the bread. 'That was a bloody nice sandwich,' he says out loud. Babs makes a beeline for his collar. She likes to suck the cuffs of his shirt, his trousers where they bag out at the knee, the hem of his coat, the collar of his winter flannelette. He smacks her across the nostrils. There'll be her silage-breath wafting up at him for the rest of the day, or the week even, until he gets around to the laundry.

In Harry's front paddock there are sixteen black and white

cows and nine black and white birds – willy wagtails. Some of the wagtails ride on the cows' backs or haunches, one grips a clump of wiggy forelock between the ears, the rest are on the ground pecking through cow pats. If it were possible to watch for long enough sooner or later there would be one bird for every cow. But it wouldn't mean anything. It would just be a pattern that's pleasing to the human eye.

The wings of a moth opening and closing over the cape weed catch the sun in a silvery flash. One grazing cow startles forwards slightly, her hind legs make clumsy haste, almost overtaking the rest of her. She settles quickly enough but the plug of fear is transferred to her sister, and then the next cow and the next, until the whole herd has felt a diluted fraction of her fear. The herd, together in the paddock, is a sponge. Feelings run like liquid in the irregular, porous spaces between each animal. Fear, alarm, anger or confusion is processed through each bovine body (added to, or diminished, depending on its nature) and flows on again, forking, branching out, to the next. In the way of a family, the herd is greater than the sum of its members. Even in a small family, three for instance, Harry has noticed this to be the case.

Alone of an evening in front of the fire Harry reads Edna's old issues of *Woman and Home*. His favourite is the romantic serial, 'A Hard Choice for Vera', which he reads over and over again. The main character is a redheaded typist. Should Vera accept an invitation from the son of the company director to play tennis? The rich and attractive young man has only ever spoken to Vera when she is seated at her desk. He hasn't noticed her misshapen foot, badly burned when she rescued her sister from a tragic house fire. All of Vera's family were killed in the fire and now she must work to support her dear little sister who shows talent as a singer and will one day be famous despite her tiny burnt hands. Nervous Vera goes off to the shops in her lunch hour to look longingly at tennis dresses. It was never going to end well; Vera dragging her monstrous foot up the office stairs day after day; Vera feeding little Eva soup in the evenings as they listen to music on the wireless. Vera with the melted foot; Eva with the melted hands. Only together do the two sisters make a whole person. What man will take them? the story asks.

Harry gets up to make himself a Milo. He shakes the kettle to check the water level. Sykes's Bag Balm is very good for burns; he has some in the dairy. Vera is so small he could easily carry her if the paddocks are too rough underfoot. And he can cut up Eva's food with the knife from the pouch on his belt. He sees picnics in the shade and perhaps swimming in the irrigation channel in the evenings – Harry floating like a log in the middle of the channel for Vera and her sister to hold on to if they lose their grip on the bank – if they become frightened in the deeper water. The water would cause the girls' blouses to cling to them, outlining the curves of their chests. Harry picks up his mug and goes to stand by the window in the front room. He can't see any lights coming from Betty's house, or from Mues's. He sucks the scum from the top of his drink and turns off the light.

Harry is riding down Saleyards Road on the Waratah when he sees Betty driving towards him. She's coming home from work. They pull up, shoulder to shoulder on the bitumen, and she winds her window down. She's wearing a spearmint-coloured cardigan he hasn't seen before.

'How's the herd?' Harry says.

Betty has to shout so her voice can be heard over the chug of the motorcycle. 'Same as always. It's hard being old. They live in their memories.'

Harry nods.

'You must have the odd memory yourself?' Betty says teasingly. 'Even a young chap like you must have a memory or two?'

They don't come with active remembering. But every so often one pushes through. Harry saves it up for her, a little awkward, a little shy in the retelling.

'Slipping into a pit of muddy water near the dam wearing a new yellow jumper ...'

'My grandfather standing at the window and waving us goodbye. Up close I didn't like how his beard grew around his lips. I didn't want to sit on his knee. They laughed at me when I put my hand over his mouth. I didn't want anyone to see his lips. But through the window he looked fine and tall. He looked like God ...'

'A horse with a white stripe running along its nostril. It put its head down to me and sniffed my face and hair. It seemed to be showing me where the milk went – that it drank milk up its nose. I thought if I was ever on my own, if my mother and father were dead, I should go to that horse ...'

'Standing in the bedroom of a house – maybe an uncle or aunt's house. The beds were pushed together to make a double. The bedspread was too small to cover both beds and I could see the sheets poking out underneath. The sheets were yellow. I chundered on the floor ...'

'Winning on a daily double at the Bendigo races then losing the betting ticket in the gents ...'

'My wife on the day we got married. Edna on our wedding day ...'

Every night after tea – always an early tea – Edna asked Harry if he'd had enough to eat.

'I'm full up to Dolly's wax,' Harry would say, patting his neck.

She warmed her hands on his belly in winter. She squeezed the pimples on his back. He fell asleep with his hand in her bush. Sometimes, just as he was getting out of the bath, she took his cock in her mouth.

There was no baby, month after month. And then she didn't like the farm. She said it wasn't the farm she didn't like, it was the shit. They were surrounded by shit. She could see it splattered across the paddocks out of every window of the house.

Monday, Wednesday, Friday: honey on toast. Tuesday, Thursday, Saturday: jam on toast. Sunday: eggs. Harry tried to be nice. It made things worse. He yelled at her; she called him a mean article. She slammed the bedroom door on him and told him to go and sleep with the shitty cows. In hindsight that was the end of it – Harry jackknifed on the couch, Edna alone in the bed. Family life ...

Harry read about a campout for the bird observers' club at Echuca, a weekend of mateship with birds. Edna said, 'Why would I want to do that?' But they borrowed a tent from her brother and lined Mues up to do the milking. On the morning they were leaving, Mues didn't arrive and Harry couldn't raise him at his house. Edna was disappointed, angry, close to tears. Harry gave her the keys to the Dodge and told her to go on her own. He took his good binoculars out of his bag and his copy of Neville Cayley's *What Bird is That?* and put them on the passenger's seat. Edna hesitated for a few minutes. She walked around the car. The cows watched them from the fence. They were agitated and started to bellow.

'Why not?' she said. 'Why bloody shouldn't I go on my own?'

In dairy country it gets dark from the ground up. The pasture, the mud on the laneways, the wetness of the land, rise to meet the linen skies. The daylight fades; then it fades again. The trees drip their black leaves; the last screech of the cockatoos. Harry stayed outside as long as he could, until the ground was murky and his feet were no longer visible. He walked cautiously in case he stumbled; his weight held back at the ankle. The kitchen door shutting behind him; his socks on the lino; water clattering into the kettle; a match struck to touch the gas … He took a Sao and ate it dry just to put something in his mouth, just to hear the sound of it breaking rudely in his head – like kindling; like words.

Edna didn't look at the birds. She followed Alec Gedge around taking notes for him and holding his camera. The letters started when she got home. He used the official stamp on the envelopes: Mr A. Gedge, President, Birds Observers' Club of Victoria, with a fantail underneath, its feet trembling because of the ink. Two months later Gedge came and collected her. Harry walked out into the paddocks when he heard the car on the road. His tongue tasted curdled in his mouth. The cows were surprised to see him out among them then, at lunchtime. She told him she needed to be on her own for a while, to develop herself and her interests. She left an address in her maiden name: Edna Orchard. Harry didn't write – except to sign the papers.

A year later, in *The Emu*:

A PAIRING OF INTEREST

*A social event of significance took place last month when our popular and energetic Secretary of the Bird*

*Observers' Club, Edna Orchard, was married to another of our esteemed members, Mr Alec Gedge. We extend our hearty congratulations to the newly minted couple and wish them many happy years on the nest together. At the wedding breakfast a series of Kodachrome slides were shown of the Easter campout at Rosebud. The slides showed an unsuccessful operation to remove tangled fishing line from the head and neck of a little tern and the autopsy of several terns that had ingested fishing line.*

At dawn Michael is pulling the tinny up the Gunbower, feeling the cold water heavy around the oars. He rows from sharply hinged elbows, his belly and shoulders held still against the wind, his slim hands folded around the oars – pressing in, pressing out, pressing back. He doesn't need to look over his shoulder; the creek ahead can be judged by the creek behind. The same thick race of water held in by a fringe of gum trees on each bank and the cumbungi dense beneath them. He edges the boat into a patch of reeds. The knife, the rod, the net and the bucket are scattered at his feet. He rinses the knife blade in the water, dries it on his shorts, pushes it into the skin of his forearm, pushes again, makes himself wait for the moment in between the slap, slap of the water against the side of the boat before the final cut. Blood leaps behind the blade. His heart flushes to attention, he feels the pain in his chest before his arm so he is able to look right into the wound; to see the softness of the flesh and the way it accepts the blade – like fruit, or cheese – like anything soft and wet that can be cut. He binds the cut with his handkerchief, leans back and rests his neck against the prow of the boat. The light is coming up quickly and with it the whine of mosquitoes moving just above the water. He closes his eyes. Iris Glassop's heavy globes bouncing, bouncing as she shoots for goal; Noreen Bird's peaked volcanoes stretching her sweater, staring straight at you as you pay for your chewing gum. The spill of flesh around Dora's armpits; the hair there, too, floating on the water when they are swimming. The twin rolls that jiggle over the top of the music teacher's bra. His sister's fried eggs. The dark outline of his mother's nipples through her nightie.

There's a clenching at the base of his cock. He braces his knees against the sides of the boat to steady himself.

The bicycle is painted black. Coming home from school Michael rides in the middle of the road as if it has been made for this purpose. He crouches low over the racing handlebars. The grey road slips away fast beneath him. Primary school finishes half an hour earlier than high school and if Little Hazel has made good time she waits for him at the intersection and asks for a dink. Sometimes he says yes. Sometimes he says no, and by the time she gets home he'll have changed and prowled around the kitchen getting something to eat and headed off to the creek or to Harry's.

Louie is curled up on the edge of the verandah. However casually cruel Michael might be to his sister, he leans down to scratch the cat under her chin and says her name as she blinks her yellow eye at him. There's wood for him to chop and the vegetable garden to weed and water, but he'll do that later – just before Betty gets home. Right now Michael likes to move through the empty house on his own. He likes the smells of the family; the stale milk in their bowls on the sink, the crumbs on the table, the jasmine that has died and dried out in its jam-jar vase. He likes the calendar from the co-op hanging on the back of the kitchen door with each square crossed out in black showing how much of the month is behind and how much is in front. With three pikelets in his hand he moves through the quiet rooms and out the back door where he pisses by the step and chews at the same time. His mouth gets so full up with the clammy dough he has to take in extra breaths to get it swallowed. He heads out across Foot Foot's paddock towards Harry's and has the sensation that he's walking back into himself. That the day at school – lining up on the asphalt quadrangle, scuffing his shoes on the wooden floors, leaning against the concrete toilet block to smoke at lunchtime – has been a kind of skimming across surfaces; that he's moved through the day without ever putting his weight down. Here, walking across the paddock, he feels his ankles soften to take account of the uneven ground. He picks his way through the clumps of cape weed and over the mounds of dirt left by the plough. There's a rhythm to it. A way of placing your feet so they are receptive to the ground beneath.

In two years' time he'll have a bitter argument with his mother about a clerical traineeship in Swan Hill and he won't be able to explain to her why it is he wants to farm.

Harry is in the machine room adjusting his new Baltic Simplex. It doesn't require lubrication. It is fitted with a control tap to suit individual cows, and an unbreakable glass observation bowl with a hygienic removable plug. The natural action of the cups supersedes all others. A free book is available by writing to: The Man in Charge, Baltic Simplex Machinery Co,

446–450 Flinders Street, Melbourne. The Simplex breaks down, on average, every fourth milking. The rubber inflations, the part that fits over the udder, require constant tensioning and repair. They crack and wear out. So if it isn't the motor or the vacuum or the lines, one of the cows will spring a leak at the peak of her let-down, causing milk to froth out of the cups and piss all over the floor. Harry has written to The Man in Charge several times since purchasing the machine, most recently in plain language. He has received three copies of the free book. The books are all the same – promotional pap. They talk the machine up and don't countenance that it might ever break down.

Michael is already in Harry's kitchen when Harry gives up and heads in. Harry has his house provisioned for all of Michael's likes. In the cupboard is Michael's special Promite, his favourite blue plate sits on the draining board, the kitchen table is stacked with books on farming, birds and cricket. Harry is surprised to find Michael standing at the draining board. He has a copy of *Woman and Home* open in his left hand. The big flat page is starting to fold over under its own weight. Harry can see it is open to 'A Hard Choice for Vera' – the page with the drawing of Vera trying on a tennis dress and looking at herself waist-up in the mirror, cheerfully unaware of how the dress pulls across her plump breasts. The top button of Michael's school shorts is undone and his right hand is down the front of his underpants. His jaw is clamped and the muscles in his neck are taut and stringy. When he hears Harry at the fly-wire door he bends over, grabbing at the front of his shorts. Harry says, 'Oh dear!' Michael drops the magazine. Harry lowers his eyes and backs quickly out of the door, noticing, along the way, that the floor is due for a sweep.

Ten minutes pass. Michael finds Harry sitting in a patch of sun on the verandah pretending to read the latest issue of the *Dairy Journal*

'The bloody New Zealanders have got there first,' Harry says, stabbing the journal with his finger.

Michael sits down next to him and picks up the binoculars from where they are resting on top of the milk ledger. 'Where first?'

'All the biggies – all the most important questions of our time: milking speeds, rotary pumps, stripping. Years of stripping every udder after every milking, meetings and circulars and standing orders on ruddy stripping, and according to the Kiwis it makes no difference at all. No increase in mastitis, no loss in butterfat production.' Harry reaches into his pocket for his pipe.

'Isn't Jones on Saleyards Road a Kiwi?' Michael asks.

'Too right he is and I've never rated him.'

Michael lifts the binoculars to his face and scans the tree-tops down by the channel. Harry taps out his pipe. It is easier not to have the boy's eyes on him.

'I've noticed you've been a bit different lately, with Dora around and that.'

Michael says, 'Mmm,' but doesn't lower the binoculars.

Harry strikes a match against the timber boards. 'Do you need an explanation of things – of things with girls? Of … details of the workings?'

Michael swallows loudly and sucks his lips. Harry takes it as a yes. They are both relieved to be alerted to a rustling in the bundy box behind the outhouse. Club-Toe is hopping around frantically; she's just dropped a skink and can't see where it has got away.

The whole family flies in formation
across the stubble of the lucerne as it burns.
A crack clean-up squadron
expertly trained, perfectly equipped
to eliminate every mouse,
skink,
beetle,
locust,
larvae,
that the fire flushes out.

I've been planning
to time the evening chorus
– when they start and how long they perform.
I'm usually in the house
and putting the kettle on.
Not sure though if I reach for the kettle
when I hear the first note,
or I just register it while I'm at the tap?
Perhaps they've trained me?
Perhaps I'm Pavlov's dog –
can't have my tea until I hear them sing?

I heard a squeal behind the dairy.
Club-Toe was on the ground with

a half-grown rat
by the neck.
She dragged it over to the fence
and bashed it senseless
against an upright.
For the next ten minutes I watched
as she ran it through her beak
– until the rat was soup inside its skin –
then she swallowed it,
in two swift gulps.

Three small beaks;
two whole,
one partial,
inside the pellet this morning.
Wagtail nestlings,
or maybe fantails.
Useful kinds of birds,
when they are alive.

I farm the land,
they farm the air.
We share roughly the same boundaries.
I buy my ground with money,
they hold their air with voice and flight.

Tiny and Club-Toe fly trapeze
between the sugar gums along the front fence.
They fly a fat line – swerving into the territory
of the scruff-headed family from Mues.
And two of Mues's birds do the same back.
Ritually crossing the line somehow marks it
– reinforces that it exists.

Just three tonight:
Mum, Dad, Club-Toe.
Tiny is missing.
They sing the evening in regardless,
bend the sound around the branches,
finish with an operatic cackle.

Why the band of dark feathers across Dad's face?
It veils the shining eye,
allows him to look without being seen
– to act in dim innocence.
On the banks of the channel I watch Dad
dive-bomb an ibis from behind.
He slams his bladed beak
into the back of ibis skull
– not to claim that bird
but so, in the instant of terror and surprise,

the tongs of the ibis beak open
and release a frog.
Dad predicts exactly where the frog will fall,
beaking it through the belly.
Why hunt when you can steal?

Tiny was killed
by the milk truck yesterday.
I found her body on the road.
She'd been cleaning moths
off the headlamps.

From a *National Geographic* at the dentist:
'The lights of a car or motorcycle
are not so deadly
as the prevailing lights
of a lighthouse.
One night's casualty list
at Eddystone, England:
76 skylarks
53 starlings
17 blackbirds
9 thrushes
and a few of
10 other species.'

It is a feature of many Australian farms
that timbered paddocks skirt the road.
We should encourage the bush
in pockets right across the land,
and along the water,
to allow safe passage
for our birds.

To my knowledge the kookaburra
does not undergo
a pre-nuptial moult.
Dad though, in early spring,
appears sprucer to my eye
with his gaudy smear of turquoise
at rump and shoulder.
And Mum is plumper, juicier
– the shape of a baked meatloaf.
Aerodynamics seems irrelevant
to these noisy tree dogs.

The sky has sufficient depth
to give each bird
its own strata,
its precise allocation of air.
Yet, like us,

they find it difficult
to live in peace.

Territorial adjustments
are constant
throughout the year.
But land grabs take place
just before breeding,
when more ground is needed to support
the expected chicks.

At breeding time a rogue bird
from a neighbouring family
will run the gauntlet
– crashing across the boundary,
hungry for territory,
for a start of their own.
The rogue is met in silence;
a flying dagger head-on,
from the side,
from behind.
The intruder is identified,
forced out,
better still – pushed to the ground
where the lower beak is ripped off.

Mum, Dad, Club-Toe
break off their
preening,
squabbling,
loafing,
to attack.
They lose themselves in the doing.
I struggle to tell them apart.
Knife-beaked,
cruel-eyed,
vicious;
there is no question
they would die for the family
– that violence is a family act.

'My lovely hair,' Betty says aloud as she goes out to collect the mail at Acacia Court. This happens sometimes: an involuntary spill of words. It is, Betty thinks, not ordinary speech where you can identify the recent thinking that produced the words, but the act of 'being spoken'. When Betty is being spoken the words fall out in false cadence like lines from a play. She glances over her shoulder. The footpath is empty and it's quiet out, except for the wind pulling at the paperbarks and giving the hydrangeas a clobbering against the fence. It is always just a few words; a snippet – sometimes a question. There are spiders in the rusty mailbox. She balances the envelopes in the crook of her arm and flicks the lid shut. Her other hand reaches up to pat a dry curl behind her ear. 'My lovely hair.'

Betty remembers an incident from the week before: Little Hazel had been trimming the feathering around Foot Foot's hocks with a pair of dressmaking scissors when she accidentally cut through the skin. Foot Foot is a heifer Harry brought over for Little Hazel to nurse because her front legs were twisted during a traumatic birth. Little Hazel brushes her and washes her and gives her physical therapy – lifting up one of her hind legs to make her take more weight up front. When the blood came up on Foot Foot's hock Little Hazel ran across the paddock to fetch Harry. She was still crying when she returned with him, holding the plug of skin and cow hair in her hand and using the back of it to wipe her nose. Michael held the heifer's head. Foot Foot didn't show any signs of distress, except for holding the injured leg off the ground. The wound was a perfect circle, the size of an apricot, with the gummy pink meat of the hock poking through. Harry requested Dettol and they got the hearth stool for him to sit on as he worked. The flies were thick. Foot Foot swished her tail from side to side to shift them. Harry asked Betty to hold the heifer's tail out of the way while he stitched. The next time the tail swished past Harry reached out for the thick swatch of cow hair and grabbed it in his fist. He handed it to Betty. She took it – the hair all tumbled and spilling messy through her fingers – and moved to the other side of the heifer's rump …

Betty puts the mail on the staffroom table and goes to the sink to wash her hands. The water from the tap at Acacia Court comes from the rainwater tank and is tea-coloured. The wind has brought rain now. As Betty soaps her hands she looks out of the window at the laundry girl stripping sheets from the line with her coat over her head. She interlaces her fingers and pushes the soap between them. Rain splatters against the window. She turns from the tap and stands drying her hands *… Here she is in the calf paddock behind the house. There is no heifer, no Michael or Little Hazel. Harry sits on the three-legged hearth stool with the needle and thread in his fingers, but it is Betty he is preparing to stitch. Betty has a cut on her knee. She stands in front of Harry holding her skirt out of the way. Her bare foot rests on his thigh. He bends close. He places one of his hands around the back of her leg to steady himself, squints, angles the needle towards her as if it is a dinky sword …*

In the daydream (but not when he really stitched Foot Foot's leg) Harry wears his glasses. He wears his glasses on Sundays for reading his bird books and doing the accounts. They have silver wire frames and he wears them close to his eyes as if he's never got comfortable with them, as if he's trying to wear them in exactly the same place the optician put them on him as a boy. Betty likes the way Harry looks out at her when he is wearing his glasses so she is not surprised he wears them in her daydream. Glasses-Harry cocks his head to line Betty up in the middle of the lens. And Betty knows that she is a little different around Harry when he has his glasses on. The idea of herself viewed through the lenses as if she is being filmed, captured in some way, makes her playful. She remembers an advertisement from a magazine: 'Things *look better behind glass …'* And then there are his eyelashes. Magnified blunt and stubbly, worn down somehow.

Betty flicks through a catalogue on the staffroom table. She steadies herself with pictures of fancy tablecloths and Christmas napkins. She knows the daydreams and the involuntary speaking are a flaw – a childish indulgence, an immaturity. It reminds her of an argument she had with her father as a child. 'Why should I eat peas?' she demanded at the dinner table. 'I like cake best. Why can't I only eat cake?'

Her father shook his head and smacked her wrist with his spoon.

'Because it will ruin you, child,' he said. 'You'll be filled up on nothing and have no room for the real food you need to eat.'

For two weeks Michael assaults Little Hazel with the word 'mucus'. He whispers it in her hair, he scribbles it on her school books, he uses his knife to write it in the gravy on her plate. He calls her 'mucus head', 'mucus brain', 'mucus face'. As soon as she becomes immune to it and stops cringing and trying to block her ears, he gives up.

Little Hazel steals the shell of a huntsman spider from the nature table at school. It is glossy and perfect with all of its legs and fangs still intact. She wraps it in her handkerchief and carries it home in the palm of her hand, being careful not to crush it. Even though it is just a shell (the spider having extracted its body to grow a larger covering), the skin on her arm goose-bumps with the thought the spider might suddenly come to life again and crawl into her hair. She puts the spider shell on the kitchen table and goes to the fridge to swig milk from the jug. Louie has been sleeping in the sun on the windowsill. Louie wakes, she yawns, she looks over at the kitchen table, notices the spider partially covered by the handkerchief and pounces. The table wobbles. Louie swipes at the spider and then looks down, baffled, as it disintegrates between her two front paws. Little Hazel says, 'Bloody hell, Louie. Thanks a bloody lot.' The spider was meant for Michael's bed.

Michael catches two large scorpions in the woodpile. He keeps them overnight in one of Harry's empty tobacco tins with the thought that they might breed, or that he can use them against Hazel. He holds the side of the tin gingerly when he prises off the lid in the morning. It's the back end you have to worry about – the sting in the tail. But there are no longer two scorpions in the tin. There is just one very fat scorpion and, on the bottom of the tin, an amputated pair of claws, open and at the ready.

On her way to school Little Hazel sees a dark knotted lump dangling from the back of an old ewe in Mues's top paddock. She climbs through the fence and by offering the ewe a few stems of green grass from the roadside gets close enough to identify the lump as the carcass of a willy wagtail. One of the bird's legs is wound firmly around and around the wool, broken just at the point where the leg bones branch into the foot – the ankle – if birds have ankles. The tough skin around the bones has kept the bird attached. It must have fought hard to free itself, thrusting with both wings, trying to push off with the other foot, breaking its leg in the struggle. The willy wagtail is basted in wool grease, its feathers are flat and oily. As the sheep turns to walk away it stumbles and the carcass bangs soundlessly against its flank.

That night Little Hazel dreams she is watching Mues take down his underpants. The dream isn't happening in a shed, but somewhere outside with green grass. She isn't frightened; she's a safe enough distance away. Mues holds up his shirt-tails, his trousers are puddled dumbly around his ankles – then she notices something she didn't notice before: Mues doesn't push his underpants down like a girl, he hooks his fingers into the elastic and lifts them out and over what's inside. Mues hooks, he lifts. A white bird flies up and out of the fabric. A white bird as stealthy as a cat has been folded in there. It shoots straight up, stretching its wings out wide to push down on the air. As it lifts, its wings cover Mues's face so Little Hazel can't see if he's shocked by this, or if he expected it. The bird, in those seconds it hovers in front of Mues's head and chest, reminds her of something. It reminds Little Hazel of the crucifixion. The bird's head is turned meekly sideways like the suffering Jesus, its wings are stretched out like arms in a wide-cut tunic, its fused tail feathers are the two feet nailed primly, one on top of the other, and covered in dripping blood. Mues and Little Hazel watch as the bird gains speed and air until it is over their heads. She wakes up.

Little Hazel thinks about the dream for several days. She thinks about the dream whenever she sees a boy or a man and she can get a clear look at the shape of his waist. It's the 'up-ness' of the thing that troubles her. She's seen Michael in the bath; she's seen pictures from the *National Geographic* and looked in a nursing textbook on the shelf at Acacia Court. It is always down, hanging down between the legs. When she was in the shed with Mues and he promised her the pony it was down at first, but then it went up. It went up like the

bird in the dream. How appalling. She feels sorry for Michael.
What horror to have an animal mechanism between your legs.
Out of sympathy she tries not to be mean to him, at least while
she remembers, at least for a few days.

A possum dies in Betty's roof. A foul, wet smell comes and goes
in drifts, worsening as the day warms up. Flies hatch through
the ceiling vents and test their new wings from room to room.
The manhole for the ceiling is in Betty's bedroom above the
wardrobe. Betty lays her dresses and blouses and uniforms and
her green winter coat with the brown collar on the bed to make
it easier for Harry and Michael to move the wardrobe and get the
ladder in place. They sprinkle perfume on a scarf and tie it over
Harry's nose and mouth for protection. Little Hazel calls him
the ceiling bandit and pats the side of his knee as he climbs past
her up the ladder. When the horrible deed is done – the anxious
crouched-walk across the beams, the scraping of the mother
corpse and her dead newborn, the scraping up of maggots (he
won't tell that to Hazel) – he's reaching out of the darkness
with his boot, feeling for the top rung of the ladder, and he
sees their three faces shining up at him like just-washed plates.

He's embarrassed by their gratitude, the cups of tea; a whisky, even, that they are offering him. He hands the stinking chaff bag down to Michael and looks away from them around the room. He wouldn't normally stare at Betty's bed, but the mound of clothes draws his eye. It is Betty's life in fabric. He recognises the work dresses, the good dresses he has seen at Christmas and birthdays, the winter coat. There's something in peach silk that must be an undergarment and then something white. At the very bottom of the pile – closest to the bed so he can't get a good look at it – is a white dress with a thick expensive lustre, like icing on a fancy cake. Harry gets a sharp ache in his gut before he even fully understands that it is probably a wedding dress; it is more than likely a wedding dress.

Harry has two baths and scrubs his hands and arms with carbolic. He is unable to eat any tea. He goes to bed early – even for a dairy farmer. He dreams of Sip with a rotting pup half out of her vagina, of his father taking a shit in a paddock of barley and squirting out a huge bubbly spray of crimson blood. In the dream, Harry and his father stand next to the circle of blood-splattered barley looking at the shit at the centre of it – a little chocolatey crescent, nothing to write home about.

The air is fresh when he goes out to milk at dawn and he takes in big gulps of it. He doesn't look into the cans before he seals them. There's a cursory glance to check for foreign matter, but this morning he's not keen to look into the milk. He can't stop seeing it in his mind though – the silky white gloss of it is fixed behind his eyes.

Four days now over a hundred. The smell of the dairy turns Harry's stomach. He wets his sheets in the bath before sleeping and wakes steamy and exhausted in the morning. He'd stay in bed, but for the cows and the sound of the tin pinging bleakly on the roof as the day heats up. Mues has asked for help with a killer so after milking Harry and Sip cross the road and meet him under the peppercorn tree where he is preparing the ropes. Mues's knives are set out neatly on the top of a forty-four-gallon drum – that's his profession showing, Harry thinks. Mues has been retired for six years now, but he still talks about his work as if it is current. Mues says a slaughterman is as skilled as a surgeon. He tells Harry about a slaughterman who conducted a successful operation on one of his children (saved himself a few bob) and another who went to the southern states of America for a lucrative career executing blacks. Harry doesn't doubt it.

Mues drags a dirty-coated ewe from the house paddock and pushes her under the tree. She's severely wool-bound so there's not much protest. They tie a rope around each of her back legs and hoist her up over a branch. Mues ties the ropes off, avoiding her stiff front legs. The change of angle confuses the old ewe. She stabs her front legs forwards as if she is expecting the ground to tilt back up again and meet her hooves. Mues grasps a handful of wool on the back of her head to stretch out her neck and slices through the jugular. Harry jumps back. The first spill rushes out in a jet; then it falls in with the beat of her heart, spurting in a regular pulse. Harry and Mues watch the blood run away from the tree. It seeks out the low ground in between the roots, flowing in fat streams.

The streams of blood stop at the exact point where the circle of shade from the crown of the tree runs out. Harry walks over and watches the place where the blood runs into the sun. The instant it touches the hot earth it solidifies, forming a bubbly purple jelly, piling up and up, on top of itself, in a frilly scum. Sip sniffs at the pudding blood. She tries licking it and biting it, but it disintegrates in her mouth. She tries a few more times and then slopes back into the shade. Harry stays put, though. It's hot out here, in the weakening shade at the edge of the tree, but he pretends to be interested in the science of what is happening – how the proteins in the blood react to the heat, causing instant coagulation. He does this because he can see that the ewe is still blinking and he'd prefer not to have to look at this as Mues is peeling the pelt off her.

Harry checks the heifers for oestrus (the effluvium, the colour and thickness of discharge), telephones the stud at Bendigo and orders seven serves of Rosedale Dreaming Fox. The next day he drives to town and collects the semen off the train. The box travels in a nest of straw on the seat beside him to protect the glassware. Every so often he takes his hand off the steering wheel and reaches across to pat the box. Egg yolk is used to cool and thin the sperm, but it doesn't keep for long. He's already yarded the little heifers and they are waiting for him when he gets home. He changes into his overalls and leads the first cow into the bails, showing her the feed of pollard in the trough. He lets her get her head down while he lathers his left arm up to the shoulder in a bucket of water laced with Dettol. When he pushes into her he folds his hand in the shape of a gun so it is as small as possible. His fingers are soft and bald, the nails trimmed especially short. And he grimaces, at the moment his hand enters her. The vagina is an empty glove. He can feel her organs pillowed through the vagina wall. Her bladder bounces up against his hand, he bats it away. He pushes deep inside her. The side of his face is pressed against her flank. He reaches for the cervix, using his free hand to thread the glass pipette so that it is resting on the nostril-rim. The semen flows forwards and then backwards a little over his fingertips. It's important to withdraw slowly, to fight the panicky feeling that his arm might get stuck inside of her, trapped by the girdles and belts of her flesh.

There are seven heifers to inseminate in one morning. Harry has bred them all and bottle-fed them and sat up through the night with them when they've had the staggers. He's been forceful at times about their heads – drenching them and checking their teeth, inoculating them with rumen. But insemination marks the start of their working lives. Each heifer will be impregnated, calve, lactate and suckle her calf. After a few days Harry will take the calf away and the new mother will join the herd. She'll learn to follow the long line of cows that walk up to the sheds every morning and evening, to approach the bails, to wait while the cow in front of her is unhooked and backed out, to tolerate the dousing of her udder, the dragging weight of the cups on her teats, the bulge of the hard rubber inflations. The dark shed with its smells of anxious shit and disinfectant and motor oil and sweet, loose milk will frighten her, but Harry will be there, and sometimes another milker – Michael or Mues – and always the thin dog shivering and standing off to one side.

Harry lets the first heifer out of the bails and admires the clean way she picks up her feet. Her mother was a fine cow. There's every indication she'll be a fine cow too.

On his next trip to Echuca to buy a part for the Waratah, Harry visits the municipal library and spends a morning in the adult section reading the famous English sex doctor, Havelock Ellis. In *Studies on the Psychology of Sex*, Harry reads about hermaphroditic slugs, the courtship rituals of spiders and a peculiar balloon-making fly.

But it is the intimate case histories at the end of the volume that interest him most. Ordinary folk from around the world, both men and women, have submitted to Dr Ellis a summary of their sexual history from their first childhood stirrings. Harry makes a few notes and stores them carefully inside his wallet. This is where he decides to start with his advice to Michael.

*When very young I was fascinated by the waterworks. I liked to pee outside and have my mother watch and remark on my* skill. At the age of four or five I remember trotting off with a cousin of similar age to see a girl's legs. I don't remember the outcome, but there was certainly some early excitement at the prospect. Around this age I got considerable gratification from rubbing myself stomach-down along my aunty's new carpet. The carpet had a floral pattern and I squirmed around from vine to vine. I remember my mother telling my aunty that I was having fun 'playing with the dog', I've never been sure if they were both aware of what I was up to. For the life of me I can't remember if my aunty ever had a dog.

I had an early distrust, fear even, of public toilets and unfamiliar outhouses. I think this was due to the foreign smells. One of my mother's friends saw me putting myself away after peeing in her garden. She said, 'Better be careful with that. A bird might get it.' I was ashamed and humiliated. I told my mother we had to leave immediately because I was sick.

Several years later the boy next door told me the basics of sexual relations between men and women. His explanation bored me – the whole apparatus seemed overly complex and technical. I dismissed it out of hand as being too ridiculous to be true.

Don't recall age at first erection, but I do remember a distinct defensive or counter-erection from very young. The member shrank inside itself with tension and local discomfort due to physical distress or revulsion. Swimming in a cold dam, undressing in front of the school nurse, visiting the dentist, having to kiss old people … This settled once erection was achieved.

Not much early interest in girls. In grade one a very fat girl sat behind me and often had her legs open when I turned around. Her knickers were grubby. I formed the impression she had an extra stomach between her legs – something like the dumpy leather pouch of a train conductor. I thought it probably opened at the top, near the navel

At the age of eight I was playing at the house of a school friend when we approached his younger sister and demanded to see her legs. We told her we needed to see if they were strong enough for her to be allowed to play our game. She refused, but agreed to let us watch her pee in exchange for a strap of licorice. I was gobsmacked at what I took to be the little mouth, the undeveloped beak, she peed with. I'm not sure what I expected, but I couldn't have been more surprised.

First erection at age eight or nine and self-handling began at this time. By the age of ten or eleven I was eager to inspect the genitals of girls and women. On a seaside holiday I attempted to look between the skirts of girls while they were swimming by lugging a piece of driftwood under the sea and using it to anchor myself to the bottom. The current made it difficult and there was often a lot of seaweed in the water. I also pretended that my concentration was being taken up with building miniature sand tunnels along the tide line so I could look up at women and girls lying, sitting and standing on the beach above me and see what I most desired to see. These attempts were clearly quite feeble, but at the time they were utterly consuming. I remember trembling with anticipation as I set out for the beach each morning.

Night pollutions started around the same time as first emissions. I never had any sense that I was doing anything wrong. I'd say to any boy now that there is nothing wrong in an empty-out. It is best not to fret about it, just get on and get it done. When I was staying with my aunty she often commented on how bright I looked in the mornings – and it was always after an emptying the night before.

By thirteen I'd be hard at it before falling asleep and back for some hair of the dog immediately on waking. Around this time a boy at school suggested we think of each other while doing it. He'd borrowed my set square during mechanical drawing and hadn't given it back. I kept thinking about the set square and was unable to produce any effect. He told me at school the next morning that he'd gone off like a rocket. I can't remember what I said. I probably lied. We (the boys) were sent to the vicar for a special talk about this time.

At fifteen I saw a fully naked woman standing behind a tree on the banks of the Gunbower wringing out her bathing costume. It was a blue-striped costume with a skirt and gilt buttons.

At sixteen I was swimming with a group of friends in the Murray near Echuca where the banks are steep and a rope ladder had been strung from a tree to help swimmers climb out. We were treading water underneath the rope ladder while a boy's mother hauled herself up the ladder over our heads. We all looked up, even her son. She had a sodden bulge at the front of her bathing suit and a riff of thick black hair springing out of the elastic around the top of each leg. Quite long tendrils of hair were flattened wetly to the insides of her thighs. I was tremendously excited (and also somehow disgusted) by this – I couldn't look her in the face afterwards without blushing, even refusing her offer of sandwiches. I've always appreciated a woman with an ample bush and I date it back to this time. The image hasn't dimmed. It still pops into my mind from time to time.

*My inclinations have always been towards the female. In Bendigo a lad started following me around at the races. He propositioned me quite blatantly in the queue at the pie van and later followed me into the public toilets. He started fondling himself at the next urinal and suggested we go back to his sister's place at Specimen Hill together where I could help him clean out the goldfish pond. I think, Michael, this may be a code for homosexual activity. I got away by saying I had a certain train to catch. Keep this in mind if you are ever seeking an excuse while on your feet. Despite not wanting to take things further with him I noticed a slight arousal when he reached out and touched my arm. I liked the strength in his hand. I liked it that someone desired me. I was seventeen at the time and covered with pimples.*

*Instances of unexpected and sudden erection: when straining hard, for example tensioning a rope; once when opening an umbrella for a woman standing waiting for a train; when teaching calves to suckle using the fingers; assisting at the covering of a mare (I was holding the mare's head and in a position to see the stallion's eye roll back into the skull at the moment of release); when one of my mother's friends touched my face at the age of fourteen. She was a big woman with an energetic bosom. I'd just seen her run across the street and she looked like she had a litter of puppies down her blouse.*

*Prior to spasm I sometimes see a very calming image of a well-irrigated pasture. I learned to whistle when very young and green has always been my favourite colour. If you want to borrow my* Woman and Home, *please take it home and store it privately in your bedroom.*

Through the night the pain alters in form like an animal seen far off in the distance. At first it is fat and hot and lodged stickily behind his ribs, then, much later, it is a sharp beak or claw pickaxing into his groin. He forces himself up and into the sheds. The chug of the Baltic is fuel for the pain. He milks and follows the cows out into the yard, moaning. Walking numbs his mind a little. He starts to lap the dairy. Sip does a few circuits with him, but she can't see the point of it. She lies down in the sun, lifts her tail at him encouragingly when he comes past again, then falls asleep. Michael finds him an hour later still walking, but buckled over, sweating and holding his side. His voice is broken into pieces. He waves Michael away with his elbow and whispers, 'Colic. Got to keep moving.'

Michael runs home to fetch his mother. He's hoping she'll tell him to call the ambulance. Betty says it's best that she examines Harry first. She trots back with Michael in her work clothes, being careful of her shoes among the cow pats. Harry tries to stand still for her, but his body has got away from him and he can't stop his knees from kicking up and down. He marches on the spot while she lifts his shirt and presses the heel of her hand against his skin. The flies are bad. He can see the dark outlines of flies on his face, like scabs. They tamper with his vision as he looks down at the top of Betty's head. She's speaking to him, she wants answers, but Harry can only moan – his voice is going the wrong way, back inside himself. Michael and Betty take an arm each and walk him slowly over to their house. Sip trots along a few yards behind them. The hardest part is sliding him through the fence. Betty tells him he's an awkward parcel and to puff through his mouth for the pain – she remembers it from childbirth.

Harry spends the day on the couch dosed up on Bex, a hot-water bottle tied to his middle with a tea towel. In the afternoon Little Hazel makes him toast with honey while Michael and Mues do the milking. Then Michael fetches his books and his glasses and he is able to sit up a little and read.

When Betty gets home from work she brings him scrambled eggs on a tray. He doesn't normally see her at both ends of the day. All her lipstick is gone now and her hair has flattened against her head. She looks old and her breath is stale from drinking tea. He can hear the children in the kitchen talking in exaggerated whispers as if they have been told to be quiet. Betty sits on the edge of the couch and takes his temperature the way mothers do – a hand on the brow. Then she smiles at him and pats his shoulder. 'I'll let you get back to your birds.' When she stands he notices the roundness of her belly, her dinner not yet digested.

Harry looks out of the window at the jasmine curling around the verandah posts. It is his cutting. He brought it over in a kerosene tin when they first arrived. Over the years he's trained it up the posts, steering it away from the gutters and towards the front door. Sometimes Sip will come back from visiting Little Hazel with a garland of jasmine around her neck and sneezing at the sweet juice of it. Sometimes he'll notice Betty with a few squashed flowers in her hair. It is worse to be here with them, in the house but separate, than to be alone. He insists on going home. Betty relents and gives him the tea strainer with instructions for its use. The stones will pass in a day or so and it is important that he collect them. She'll put them in the outgoing pathology at Acacia Court and get them tested for anything sinister.

The pain is duller now. He carries Betty's tea strainer in his pocket and mainly remembers to piss through it; increasing his proficiency at hitting the mesh rather than the rim and avoiding splatter.

It's nearly a week later; he's taking his last piss of the day under the sugar gums, looking up at the kookaburras engaged in a bout of family bickering, when the two stones wash out of his cock. The smaller, oval-shaped one could be a piece of the larger stone that has chipped off on its long trail through his organs. They are not really like stones at all, more lumps of hardened molasses rolled in chaff. He double-boils Betty's tea strainer and places the stones in a clean Vegemite jar on the kitchen windowsill. In the morning he notices they have exuded a little watery milk and are stuck to the bottom.

As he walks across the paddock with the jar in his hand he thinks of all the things he has walked across the paddock to Betty's with – milk, binoculars for Michael, tools, guttering, records, brake oil, Christmas presents, an orphan calf, cuttings from the garden, various veterinary ointments, articles from magazines for Little Hazel, lemons, and now an intimate letter for Michael tucked into his sock. He looks at the stones through the glass. This is what I gave birth to, he thinks. They look obscenely sexual – testicular perhaps. He feels disconsolate and ashamed.

Just before breeding
the family tilts
on its axis.
Dad and Mum are selfishly involved.
There are outings together
around the territory;
the viewing of several nest options,
although,
for as long as I have known,
they always use the same hollow
in the red gum behind the dairy.

Club-Toe skulks;
flies solitary around the border,
sometimes ventures into rival country.
Or she just sits, torpid,
beak down,
eyes glazed.
I can only interpret it
as glumness.
An understanding, perhaps,
that she's missed the boat again
and won't be breeding this season.

A honeyeater,
tongue drunk

on nectar,
sleeps it off
beneath a flowering gum.
Until Dad, perched above,
notices the jerky
intoxicated cycling of its twiggy legs.
That's supper sorted.

More border antics
with the neighbours today.
Mum and Club-Toe fly between
a sugar gum and the bundy box
watched by two scruff-heads from Mues's.
One at a time
Mum,
then Club-Toe,
launch from a branch of the sugar gum
and fly towards a scar
on the box
doing an open-winged
bellyflop into it,
before pushing off again.
This goes on for some time
– the birds taking turns,
crossing in mid-air,

until they stop
and watch politely as the neighbours
mount their own display.

Kookaburras
are more likely to fly into windows
during the breeding season.
The mirrored reflection
is mistaken for an intruder,
and attacked,
without thought for personal safety
– or any concern
for the cost of glass.

Dad is attentive in the breeding weeks,
he takes Mum on outings around the farm,
chatters, brings her beetles,
jollies her along
while she ripens.
Until, this morning,
I hear her keening in agony
and rush out of the kitchen ready for rescue
to see her being
bored,
skewered,
on a low branch of the angophora.

Dad grips her neck and back,
tries to fly himself
inside of her.
The force of it tips them from the tree
and they tumble
in a double-winged free fall
to the ground,
where he pushes her against the cape weed.
And when he's finished
flies away,
in silence.

They work in pairs
against a fairy wren.
Dad buzzes the nest,
the wren throws herself on the ground
to draw him away.
She pluckily performs her decoy
– holding out her wing as if it is broken.
A small bird on the ground
is easy picking,
Club-Toe finishes her off.

Mum went down in the dam today.
She miscalculated on the descent

and instead of braking
to pull a dragonfly
from the surface of the water,
she went in
and almost didn't come out again.
This mistake must be easy enough to make
at the best of times,
even easier when you are egg-heavy
and hungry with it.

There is a trick they do,
an optical illusion,
when a goshawk flies overhead,
or a kite.
They sit perfectly still;
their head feathers erect,
their beaks wide open.
It breaks up the plump
bird-outline
and from above
gives the impression of a stick.

The rule of thumb
is to catch something
of a size to be swallowed,

or better still,
steal it.
A good-sized copperhead
down by the channel,
its jaws blocked up nicely with a rat,
is defenceless
– just a length of muscle.
Mum and Dad work together
harassing the snake about the head,
stabbing at its eyes.
Dad, a fat jockey on its back,
grasps with his claws
and drills with his beak
until,
in exasperation,
the snake drops the rat.
Dad lifts instantly,
Mum a second later,
kicking the rat up into her beak.

I've noticed a vibration just before the call,
as if the air is being tuned
to take delivery of the sound.
Perhaps I'm listening
too keenly

– perhaps my ears tense
as soon as they open their beaks
because I know
the air is about to flower?

A fracas in the bundy box.
Dad again.
The air is no good for sex,
you need gravity,
you need a sense of weight
and purchase.
This time I leave them to it.
I'd prefer he didn't hurt her,
or at least,
I'd prefer not to see it.

Father Mulvaney comes to Acacia Court once a month to bless the Catholics. He's from Dublin, via Swan Hill. Little, like a jockey, with dyed black hair and sharp lines on his tanned face, he talks non-stop and does a bit of singing and enjoys a port with lunch. Betty is cleaning the dentures with baking powder when he comes up behind her and slaps her on the rump. 'Don't get bitten by those choppers, my lovely,' he says. He takes one of her wet hands in his. 'You've beautiful hands, Mrs Reynolds.' He strokes the back of her hand right down to her fingers like he's patting the head of a dog, then he turns it over and stares down at the palm.

'Did you know that the crucifixion wasn't ever really through the hand? It's a misunderstanding that we think that. When Jesus says to Thomas, "Observe my hands," he really meant, "Observe my wrists." A nail driven through the palm will be dragged out between the fingers by the weight of the body. So the crucifixion nails were hammered in here – just here between the small bones of the wrist.' He pushes his thumb into Betty's pulse. 'And how are those children of yours – a boy and a little girl, wasn't it? Have they been warming up the pews lately?'

This is why Betty left the city. To get away from the insinuators; to give the children some air around them, to put some distance between the woman she is now and the ardent girl of her past. They don't need the church, she's sure of that – they have each other. Little Hazel has Foot Foot now, and Michael has Harry and the farm. Betty is aware of the talk behind her back when she comes to town – her children referred to as 'Betty's bastards'. If anyone ever said it to her face she'd crucify them – through the wrist or through the hand.

Betty's old men die in batches. Dennis Popp goes first, then Bill Sickle. The children know there is a funeral because she takes her good shoes to work in a brown paper bag. Flowers come home, and fruit or cakes that have gone uneaten. Relatives give her gifts – cheap talcum powder and soap – or they give her dead men's things they can't be bothered taking home. Michael and Little Hazel are wary of combs with broken teeth, of faded bed rugs and pencil stubs that look well licked or as if they've spent time behind an aged ear. Michael and Little Hazel don't hesitate to tell Betty that she smells bad sometimes after work.

After Bill Sickle's funeral Betty cleans out the trunk beneath his bed. There's half a bag of chaff in there and the crankshaft for a '48 Holden; the harmonic balancer at the end is wrapped in a Masonic towel. There is also his dead wife's wedding dress with a note on it, in Bill's shaky handwriting, *'For Betty'*. Betty takes it home and puts it in her wardrobe with her good winter suit and her day dresses and uniforms because she doesn't want to throw it out and she doesn't know what else to do with it. It's not as if she was a stranger to him. She was his lunchtime-wife for a good four years.

The winking owl is on the washing line again as Betty rinses her cup before bed. It looks over its shoulder to Foot Foot's paddock behind and Betty is surprised to see it move so graciously, all the time its eyes tracking like searchlights. Tonight it lifts one claw and transfers something small to its beak. A baby mouse, perhaps, or a beetle.

Shopping after work, Betty falls in the rain. Her heels slide out from under her on the wet timbers of the verandah in front of Oestler's Fruit and Veg. She goes down heavy, face first; puts her tooth through her lip, bleeds a lot of orange sticky blood over her uniform. Clive Oestler sees her fall and rushes out from behind the counter. As he bends over, a big dirty potato rolls out of his apron pocket and hits Betty on the head. He can't stop apologising and Betty has to reassure him over and over again that she hardly felt the potato (it's true, hitting the ground was much more painful). He hurries back inside the shop and carries out a stool and insists that Betty sit on it, in the middle of the verandah, while she gets herself together. Betty perches on the edge of the stool, the back of one hand pressed to her lower lip to staunch the bleeding and the other hand clasped around the potato that Clive seems to have forgotten about in all the commotion. She sits. A few people walk past and look at her sideways. She tries to smooth out her breathing. She chooses a tree over on the bank of the Gunbower to look at so she won't have to meet anyone's eye.

After a little while she stands and picks a wet leaf off her leg where it has stuck to her stockings. She goes inside to thank Clive, buys some tomatoes that she doesn't need and walks back to the car without the rest of the shopping. The windscreen wipers aren't working properly and as she drives home the sound of them scraping across the glass sets her teeth on edge. She has a strong urge to pull over to the side of the road and rest her head on the steering wheel, but it won't do. She puts her foot down. The tyres slap through the deep puddles on the side of the road. She thinks about what they'll have for tea and about getting her dress in to soak quickly so that it doesn't stain.

Harry likes to use the word 'nippy' in Betty's company. Betty estimates that between 1951 and 1953 Harry says 'nippy' to her on over a hundred occasions – many of them not even during the winter. He says that the wind is nippy, the air is nippy, it is nippy in the shed, paddock, garage, kitchen, main street, post office and butcher's. Various places other than Cohuna are nippy, or so he's heard – London, for instance; Iceland, Latvia, the Sahara Desert at night. Even Bendigo, Harry says, can be a bit nippy for his liking. Some of the cows get fractious when the weather is nippy. Milk yields drop in nippy conditions. His dermatitis is always worse when it's nippy. Betty knows it's coming, she's used to it now. In the early days she dropped her eyes and crossed her arms over her chest. Now she looks at him dead-set. She puts her shoulders back and hoists them up a little higher. She imagines herself as Mae West. Mae-West-Betty would say to Harry, 'Don't beat around the bush, Harry. This is what you want. Come over here and get it.' And she would lean forwards and tip her breasts out of her bra, the nipples linty and crumpled, but pointing straight at him.

Podiatry or office work. Little Hazel pulls a face. The verdict of the vocational guidance officer has been sent home to Betty on a slip of pink paper. Little Hazel doesn't like feet.

Old people's feet are disgusting. She'd been hoping for jockey, or explorer. Her breasts are coming in. She checks them each morning when she gets dressed. She wears two singlets to push the nipples flat. Last week a mouse ate the crotch out of the knickers she left on the floor.

In the winter school holidays some of the children in Little Hazel's class are going on a bus trip with their mothers and fathers to see the snow at Mount Baw Baw. Little Hazel has never seen the snow. On the school holidays Little Hazel stays home with Michael or goes to Acacia Court with Betty.

Walking through the back door of Betty's house, Little Hazel's sleep-out is on the left, Michael's is on the right. The sleep-outs are a closed-in section of the verandah with unlined timber boards halfway up the walls and louvred aluminium windows above them. Green paint has been slapped on top of the boards, but many tufty, barky bits show through. In the summer it is good enough. In the winter Little Hazel buries her head under the blankets to get to sleep and often wakes in the morning with an earache from the draught.

Harry is wary going into Little Hazel's sleep-out. He is anxious about being confronted with 'girl's things'. But there is only the messy bed, a pile of clothes on a chair, a little table with her drawing pencils, some pictures of mudlarks thumbtacked to the wall, a doll, a rabbit knitted out of grey wool, and a diorama of the forest at night made from painted Cornflakes boxes. Harry does his work carefully, starting from the ceiling. He uses binder twine to construct a hammock for the silky fibres of the kapok and then spends a long time winding more kapok around the twine so it doesn't show. He tries to imagine how the kapok-snow might have landed on the windowsill and bed and table and floor if it had really fallen from the sky. He takes care to 'snow' the diorama; the white looks very striking against the black paint. As a finishing touch he gently snows the ears of the rabbit and even places a wisp on its tiny snubbed nose.

When Little Hazel returns from taking Foot Foot for her afternoon walk Harry is already back at home and setting up for the milking. She opens her bedroom door to throw her jumper in so she won't be in trouble when her mother gets home. Everything is white; the ceiling is a hummocky white mass, the floor, the bed, the table. The room is covered in a soft, quiet, spidery whiteness. Little Hazel put her hands to her face in surprise. She notices how the whiteness muffles the sharp shapes and edges of everything it covers. The objects in her room seem more important, more symbolic and statuesque, in their blank pallor. There's a gentleness about it too.

Michael, and later Betty, also stand quietly at the door and admire the snow. Betty buys Harry a new pillow at the co-op as a replacement although he insists he used an old one and has no need of it.

Harry comes around a bit those school holidays. He often has to borrow something or return it. Sometimes Little Hazel pretends Harry and Sip are formal guests and shows them through to the front room where they drink tea together and read books. They look at a pictorial gazette of the *New Age of Transportation* Little Hazel borrowed from the school library. There are pictures of modern cars and trains and aeroplanes. One of the pictures shows a gigantic car ferry that travels between England and France. A huge mechanical ramp leads to the inside of the ship where cars of different models are lined up, some with picnic baskets tied to their roofs. Well-dressed families stand around the cars, the children are bare-legged but in the fitted coats and socks-with-sandals of the foreign rich.

'Young Sip here would like to go to France on a car ferry,' Little Hazel says lazily, stroking Sip's ears. Sip hears her name being spoken. She blinks in recognition and licks her needley teeth. Harry and Little Hazel laugh at her so she gets up haughtily and takes herself over by the window where there is a patch of sun.

When Harry comes the next day, Little Hazel tells him that she dreamed about the ferry. In the dream Betty's Vauxhall is in the hold of the ferry and Betty has forgotten to put the handbrake on (not unusual) so all night, as the passengers sleep in their bunks above, Betty's car has rolled backwards and forwards with each sway of the ferry. Betty's car hits the car in front of it, and then the car behind it, until the force of this loosens the brakes of all of the cars, causing them to slide into one another like marbles on wet glass. In the dream Harry and Betty and Little Hazel and Michael are having breakfast in the ferry's grand dining room with tinkling chandeliers and runny eggs. Only Little Hazel knows the carnage that awaits them as soon as the ferry docks and the gigantic ramp is let down. She wants to warn her mother, but her mouth is stuck with egg. And there's a stranger at the table with them – a woman who looks a bit like Michael's friend Dora, but has the wrong hair. Whenever Little Hazel tries to speak this woman interrupts.

'I woke up feeling as if something bad will happen and I'm not going to be able to stop it.'

Harry makes a noise at the back of his throat. A calming noise he makes when the calves are frantic for their bottles.

'Do you think I should tell Mum?' Little Hazel asks. Her face is red. She sniffs and rubs her nose.

Harry puts his hand on the girl's shoulder. Then he takes a handful of hair that's fallen from her ponytail and tucks it back behind her ear. 'It's alright,' he says. 'Settle, petal. It's alright there.'

At school number 2502, Cohuna, Little Hazel's teacher sets aside fifteen minutes on a Friday afternoon for the class to write up their nature diaries. There is a prize at the end of the year for the best diary, with marks awarded for composition and illustration. The boys are doing a comic strip – *Eagle Versus the World*. Out of all of the boys only one of them can draw. Little Hazel brings pressed leaves and flowers from home and traces around them on the page, but they break apart and it takes too long to colour in the outlines, so she writes. She takes some advice from Harry and she tries to write what she sees.

## HAZEL REYNOLDS'
## NATURE DIARY

*February*
*When we came back to school we moved into the top*
*classroom. There is a bird table outside the window. We take*

turns filling up the dishes with water and birdseed. Already there have been rosellas a butcher bird and a thrush.

It was a very hot day to-day. There were 17 magpies on the grass outside the window. At lunchtime our teacher put the sprinkler on and in the afternoon there were 63 magpies on the grass. It looked like they were having a conference.

The thrush comes to the bird table all of the time. Our teacher can get very close to it and we watch from the window not making the smallest noise to frighten it away.

We saw the thrush on the bird table so much because there are actually two of them. There is a baby thrush and a mother thrush. The baby thrush will take a worm from our teachers hand.

March
To-day there were many crimson rosellas at the bird table. Our teacher calls them red lories. They have strong beaks and are a great bane of life for our fruit growers. All of the birds are happy when there are rosy tips in the sky.

Yesterday mother thrush hopped through the window. She flew around the classroom. The boys stood on the desks and took the model of the solar system down in case she got tangled in it. She hopped on the teacher's table and she gave her a worm.

*April*

*A kind lady said she would do the bird seed over the easter holidays. There are no birds at the bird table now that we are back. Our teacher said they will thicken up soon.*

*Some girls playing on the swing found a little budgie with blue feathers. Its beak has grown into a hook. It has escaped from a cage. The girls are allowed to keep it in their classroom until someone comes to get it.*

*Our teacher can get the mother thrush to come in the window when she whistles. She hops on the backs of our chairs. She tried to eat some spaghetti on Shirley Timms collage but it had gone dry.*

*May*

*This afternoon mother thrush sat on my hand. I have a tiny scratch mark like from a twig.*

*Mother thrush came into the classroom four times to-day. She got a worm each time. When she comes in we stop our work to watch her and see what she will do.*

*To-day our teacher had three red lories feeding from her hands. She wasn't quick enough with seed for the biggest one and it gave her a bad nip on the finger. We got the first aid box from the office.*

*It is cold today so all the windows are closed. We were*
*having our spelling test and our teacher was walking up*
*and down the rows saying the words and putting them in*
*sentences. We heard a bang on the window. We didn't know*
*what it was but Ron Hodge went outside and the mother*
*thrush was dead under the window. Some of the girls cried*
*then we buried her.*

*June*
*A jacky winter came to the bird table to-day. It is a melodious*
*bird with a many magic lilting notes.*

*Our teacher told us a story about two kookaburras. The*
*kookaburras had a nest in a tree hollow near her house.*
*The top of the tree where they were nesting came down*
*in a big storm. The next day the mother and father*
*kookaburra used their beaks to try and hammer a hollow*
*further down the tree, but the wood was too hard and they*
*gave up. In the afternoon she saw them flying around a*
*tree further down the road near the saleyards. They were*
*harassing a big old possum and it worked. He got sick of*
*the noise and the pecking. When he moved out the*
*kookaburras moved in. Our teacher says kookaburras are*
*opportunists.*

*Some magpies have started swooping already. Two boys were swooped near the bridge on the Leitchville Road and one had blood coming out of his hair. They mainly swoop boys.*

Harry drains the oil on the Waratah. It's a complicated job due to the awkward position of the sump plug. He has the front end of the motorcycle hoisted over the rafters in the dairy to get some rise on the mid-section and set the oil moving. A quick ride around the farm warms the oil up, but by the time he's got the bike in position it's cooling again. Harry crouches down and watches the thick liquid pool around the lip of the plug. Oil has something of the herd about it – piling back up on top of itself, wanting the familiar, being reluctant to spill forwards into the new unlubricated space. He rocks the bike back and forth to loosen the oil within, to make it run faster. The oil trickles out of the plug. He shakes the bike again. The oil is sluggish, it doesn't want to run. He's getting frustrated. Harry wants to kick the bike, but he tries to lift the whole weight of it in his arms and jolt it in the air instead. It swings viciously on the rope; the handlebars jackknife sideways one way and then the other. When he leans over to check the oil pan, to see if it is finally filling up, the back tyre catches him on the side of the head and neck. It clocks him hard, bounces away with the impact and comes back for another go. Harry has his arms up by then, protecting his face. He lets himself fall over sideways so he's flat against the bricks. The bike swings above him. He lies still, fingers his cheekbone for a break and rubs his temple where the tyre tread has broken the skin. The oil drips from the swinging bike and traces a figure-eight pattern on the ground – some of it within the pan, some of it outside. It'll need shovelling up and covering with soil so the cows don't slip in the morning. Harry puts that out of his mind for now. He lies still and listens to the sound of the rope sighing where it is pulled tight around the rafters. He watches the oil making its pattern; slower, slower, slower. He puts out his hand, feels the oil slide across his thumb and seep between his fingers. 'Yes,' he says. And, 'Yes,' when it comes past again.

Harry takes his sore head over to Betty's for an assessment. She has a pot of something for bruises – arnica? They've just finished tea. Dora from the poultry farm is making up the foursome at the kitchen table – completing the family axis – making it square. Dora, Betty and Little Hazel are hunched over a magazine. It's a picture of young Queen Elizabeth smiling with her neat, chalky teeth. Dora traces the Queen's hat with her fingertip – it's a flat oval-shaped cloche pinned across the middle of her head like a saddle. Dora says she's thinking of knitting something similar. Harry comes in for a closer look. Nobody has noticed the blood on his temple. 'You could achieve the same effect with a placemat, or a large pikelet, even,' Harry says.

Little Hazel giggles. Dora closes the magazine and takes a handful of Michael's shirtsleeve in her hand.

'Come on, you, we've got homework.' She leads Michael towards the front room.

Betty looks at Harry. 'They're "study-buddies",' she says flatly.

Harry and Betty hold each other's eye. They don't like the sound of this: it's American, it's show-offy – it's not their way.

Harry has no idea what makes a girl like Dora tick. He hasn't even imagined her naked. He sees her and Michael go down to the channel to catch dragonflies after school while he's grubbing out thistles along the bottom track. There's a lot of shenanigans with the long handle of the net and the girl's dress. She's a thin girl with big knees. She picks her feet up without thought. She turns her head immediately when she hears the kookaburras in the trees. She talks easily. She laughs loudly. She's a running tap, Harry thinks, a swig of water.

Not like Betty. His Betty is heavier, more complicated. Betty meanders within herself; she's full of quiet pockets. The girl Dora might be water, but his Betty is oil. You can't take oil lightly. It seeps into your skin. It marks you.

Harry and his mother are staying with Aunty Bev at Kangaroo Flat. His mother and his aunt have gone shopping together in the big emporiums of Bendigo. They always come back exhausted from these trips; parched for a pot of tea and needing to soak their feet in basins of hot water. Seven-year-old Harry has been left on his own for three hours. He has the front garden to weed and two encyclopaedias he's brought from home – J–L and S–T. Three hours is three viewings of the wooden bird that springs from his aunt's cuckoo clock. A set of plaster ducks fly up the wall of the good room. Above the mantelpiece, its weights dangling like polished acorns, hangs the cuckoo clock. At four minutes to ten Harry wipes the grass grease from his hands on his shorts and pushes the door of the good room open. Four minutes. Harry stands to attention in front of the clock. He quickens his breathing, puffing in and out to speed things up. Time, in Harry's understanding, is measured in the body. It has something to do with the lungs and the taking in and expelling of air. At school they march on the spot and are ordered to take long deep breaths; in one-two, out one-two. Breathing is numbers – time is numbers. Grown-ups seem to know the time within themselves. They are always announcing it – time for bed, time for dinner, time for chores. Clocks, young Harry thinks, are reminding devices for when people forget, or when they wake up from sleeping and have not been paying attention to the ins and outs of their lungs. Harry believes that by breathing faster he can make the four minutes in front of the cuckoo clock go quicker. He sniffs and sniffs, gets a little air-drunk and has to sit on the edge of one of the velvet chairs. The clock ticks on and on. Finally he hears the whirr and grind of the clock's gears running through their pre-call machinations. Then the miniature stable doors – more suited really to a horse than a bird – jerk open and the wooden bird shoots out on its zigzagged arm.

The bird's head is perfectly round so it looks babyish, a mere chick. Its triangular beak opens and closes. There are two wheezy blasts of sound. A pause then it starts again, the splitting beak, the two-tone call. Harry strains upwards to get a closer look at the cuckoo – but this takes him further away from the sound. He realises that the sound isn't coming from the bird at all, but from somewhere below, inside the case of the clock, or further back even, inside the wall. He pushes one of the wicker chairs over to the mantelpiece and using all the strength in his arms lifts the heavy clock from the wall. He places it carefully on the hearth rug and opens the latch at the back of the case. There's a bronze pendulum the size of a soup spoon and underneath it layers of interconnected cogs and springs. At the very bottom of the clock case, in each corner, is a leather bellows. Harry pushes one of them with his finger and it makes the second half of the cuckoo sound, but with a puffed sigh at the end. The lungs of the cuckoo bird are not inside the bird itself. They are just a mechanism within the clock. The cuckoo clock is an act of ventriloquism; a callous device – the mute bird skewered to the thrusting arm – forced hour after hour to repeat its trick. Harry is unable to lift the clock back up to its hook on the wall. He closes the case. The pendulum has detached and at least two springs have gotten away and bounced under the china cabinet. He turns the clock the right side up, so the bird can get out if the doors open again, but he doubts they will.

He's not sure how much time has gone by now and how long it will be before his mother and his aunt come home. His legs are heavy as he goes out into the garden to finish the weeding. It's getting hot. He crouches so low in the grass a swarm of rubbishy gnats fly into his face. He can feel the tears concentrating inside him, rising in a thick wad, and the smell of bleach that goes with them. He thinks he might as well cry now, the crying will have to come. There will be the disappointment on his mother's face and his shame at that. But there's something more, too. He feels like he has lost something. He tries to slow his breathing now, to slow everything down, to give himself more time, but the tears have made his nose run and he's having to suck great gulps of air in. He's the cause of the trouble and he's bringing it on himself fast.

Harry takes Michael out behind the dairy where a few stray clumps of phalaris have self-seeded in the boosted soil. Michael's hands are balled in his pockets; he scuffs the soil with the toe of his boot.

'Come on in, lad. Get a look-see.' Harry kneels down in front of a small plant. Sip darts in and licks his beard. Harry shoulders her aside. Three or four long seed heads have sprouted from within the tight mound of tangled stemlets. Harry takes his penknife, cuts the long stems and tosses them aside. The shorn plant with its even fleece instantly has the look of an animal about it.

Michael moves up behind Harry. He looks over his shoulder so he won't have to make eye contact or get distracted by the expression on Harry's face. Harry clips and shapes. He brushes a fly away from his mouth and clears his throat.

'Strong and wiry, Michael, the female pubic bush. Coarse. Nothing like the soft hair of the head. I've always thought of it more as fur than hair. Similar colouring can be expected. Dark hair, dark bush; mousy hair, mousy bush and so on, and it'll all go to grey in the end with senile decay. Not that you have to worry about that for a while, eh?'

Michael makes a brief noise of agreement behind his teeth. Harry pushes on.

'Why then? Why then a thick bush of hair directly over the female genital opening? In my reckoning the answer is climate. The bush creates a protective warmth, a humid environment for the essential sexual tissues beneath it. See the plant, Michael?' Harry motions roundly with his hands. 'The plant is in constant conversation with the soil beneath it. The plant funnels in water and provides shade and nutrients that keep the soil moist and fertile. First rule of farming, Michael?'

Michael moves his head slightly to indicate that he doesn't know.

'First rule of farming, Michael, is keep your ground covered. And I'd extrapolate it is much the same with this. Remove the bush and the whole – whole … mechanism will dry out beneath it.'

Harry takes Michael's hand in his and places it on top of the phalaris.

'Don't just be tempted to stay on the surface. You have to push in.' He turns Michael's hand sideways and uses it like a knife to chop through the leafy stems to the soil below. 'This is where the riches are. Notice how the soil is moist beneath the plant, but not in the surrounding area?'

They stand up, Harry absentmindedly still holding Michael's hand. A cow bellows in the paddock behind them. Harry reaches out and rests his boot on the bush.

'The pubic bush. A bloody miracle. And it has no sense of gravity. Despite being stuck halfway up in the air most of the time, from what I can see it doesn't droop.'

Harry favours the demonstration, the practical approach, but he finds it difficult to discuss his own experiences with Michael. Some intimate topics are better tackled in the evening with a cup of Milo, a sharpened pencil and several sheets of Basildon Bond.

*I remember this from the early days with Edna. I was making
a sandwich in the kitchen and she'd just got up from a nap.
It was late afternoon. She had a piece of crochet wrapped
around her shoulders and just her underslip on. She propped
herself up on the kitchen counter and watched me collecting
the paraphernalia – knife, meat, pickles, dripping, plate,
bread. Each time I walked past her she put her bare leg out
and touched me with it; sort of wiped it against me. I didn't
pay much attention. Ate my sandwich, rinsed the plates. Put
everything away shipshape. Then I went over to give her a
friendly peck and she had me. Legs around me like a vice,
pulling me in to her and her eyes – I noticed her eyes – all
glassy, turned in on themselves (remember Babs when she
had the staggers?). Despite the shock of it I wasn't averse.
(I can't think, Michael, of many times in my life when
I've been averse.) She pulled her slip up and without the
hindrance of underpants I slid my fingers between her legs
(under the furred pubic mound the skin clefts and splits much
like the bifurcation of stone fruit, only deeper), into a slick, a
drenching, of sex oil. The internal skin of the female organ is
pitted with oil-producing glands that release on arousal. In my
experience a slight dampening is the usual state of play, but
this particular afternoon Edna was irrigated full-bore. I won't*

go into the mechanics of what followed, the point of interest here is the timing and quantity of secreted oil. My reckoning is that it was the sandwich. The connection between sex oil and saliva is obvious. The role of the male in keeping the female well nourished goes back to the ancients, but over the years we've drifted away from the biology of it. Feeding the female prior to sexual congress triggers the secretions of saliva and of sexual oil that prepare her for the downstairs menu. This time with Edna, she wasn't even eating. Just watching me down that sandwich was enough to turn the tap. The practical advice for you, Michael, is to keep the lass in question grubbed up. (I add that it doesn't work in reverse. Edna eating, or drinking, produced no appreciable change in my equipment.)

Is it water? No. It is thicker than water, but thinner than oil. And it doesn't wash away with soap. Sticks to the skin so the smell (muddy) can be carried for days – especially on the pads of the fingertips and under the nails.

Harry and Michael take a breather from spreading manure in the bottom paddock. Harry takes out his pipe and goes through the rituals of emptying it and cleaning it and filling it. He gets it ready for lighting regularly, he's often on the verge of lighting it, but he rarely smokes. The herd stares at them intently through the fence. Pauline lifts her hind hoof and wobbles as she doubles around, attempting to scratch her neck.

'See that cow?' Harry says, pointing at her.

'Yep,' Michael says.

'She's a fine example. Well covered. It's a good sign in a female too. A good question to ask yourself, Michael – is she well covered?

Michael's eyes widen. He looks around in surprise. Harry continues, his voice in a firmer register now as he warms to the topic.

'Modern dresses are appalling. I have a mind to write to the magazines or the pattern makers. Women are not fields of flowers, or ghosts, or clouds, or presents tied up with bows, or the low-waisted thing like a ruddy flag that droops across the hips. The dress should give a man some indication of the basic shape of the female it contains. Is she well covered? What of the rump and bosom? The thin frame is to be avoided. It's alright in a girl because you know she'll get over it, but never in a woman. The female was made to carry flesh. It's shorter, closer to the ground, lower centre of gravity. Look at Pauline.' Harry waves his pipe in her direction. 'The hips should be capacious. They should spread. Think of how we choose a

milker at the sales – lean against her and see that she isn't
going to collapse. Front on your woman needn't take up too
much space, but side on she needs some depth about her.'

Michael stamps his boots and edges off towards the tractor.
Harry sucks on his pipe a few times to clear the stem.

'Back to work is it, then?'

What is the fixative that causes one memory to congeal and
set, while others dissolve? As Harry puts the tractor away the
afternoon sun on the back of his neck puts him in mind of
the heat of his teenage summers; a fierce, roasting heat. He
remembers having just turned fifteen and riding the hay …
he's high on top of a full dray, lying on his back with his hat
over his face. He's as tall as a man, but he hasn't found his
strength yet. A day's loading in the sun leaves him dizzy with
exhaustion. Next to him one of the labourers is hitching a
lift into town. His name is Vernon, but they call him Ruby.
He's a weedy redhead with a crop of old acne scars across
his face like drained volcanoes. The scars get in the way of
Ruby's facial expressions so he seems slow in his reactions.
Perhaps generally slow. He's nineteen, but he looks younger.
They don't talk during the loading – it's too hot and the
work is crushing. Each man just does his job, calling out

the briefest of communications and instructions to the others – up, right, left, heave, twine-up, smoko and the number of bales needed to finish a row. Harry keeps himself especially separate because he hates the work. His hands are raw, his arms ache, his eyes smart from the sweat running into them and there's the constant threat of snakes. He figures that if he starts to talk he'll probably cry.

Harry is nearly asleep when he feels Ruby's boot against his leg.

'Hey, Harry?'

Harry slides his hat off his face and looks across at Ruby.

Ruby is lying on his side, smirking. The smirk and the pressure of the hay on the side of Ruby's face have pushed some of the scars together, forming sideways cracks between them.

'Hey, Harry, been spending much time with Mother Palmer and her five daughters?' Ruby puts one hand up in the air as he says this and wiggles his fingers.

'Um?' Harry hopes the sound he has made will pass for understanding, or that Ruby will think he's asleep. He hears Ruby roll over onto his back and the sound of him unbuckling his belt and pushing his trousers down.

'You don't mind if I knock the top off this, then?'

No answer is needed. Ruby spits into his palm and starts to masturbate. Harry sleeps. When he wakes the sun has slipped down behind the dray and the heat has eased, but he still feels addled and groggy. He thinks about rolling onto his belly and crawling over to the edge of the load to see how far they have travelled and to call down to his father for the water bag, but the sun has sucked the life out of him. He wishes the summer over, wishes the work was done with forever. He makes a promise to himself. Farming isn't out of the question, but not grains. He'll stay closer to town, do something with animals and have regular money and regular folk to talk to. He looks over at Ruby. He's asleep with his mouth open and his trousers still bunched around his knees, his spent cock points listlessly towards Harry and nods in time with the motion of the dray.

Harry pisses on the lemon tree just after midnight. He's on the way home from drinking beer and playing cards under the electric light in Mues's kitchen. It is a relief to be out in the air again. He looks up at the dark forms of the trees with the night sky showing through behind them. The eucalypts' thin leaves are painterly on the background of mauve sky – like black lace on pale skin. An image of an old-fashioned bodice pulled tight across a woman's bust with the skin rising puffily between the thread comes to mind. There's an early, jerky, sense memory – a close-up of skin in between lace. A tongue, Harry's infant tongue perhaps, reaches out to taste the skin's oily sweetness and is disappointed that the lace has no special flavour of its own. He's not sure now if he's remembering or imagining, but he can sense an area of stippled inflammation protruding from the lace – a nipple that's got free. The nipple is the same rude pink he saw inside his mother's mouth when she coughed or yawned. The memory and its associations are both alarming and exciting. He finishes pissing but doesn't bother to button his trousers. He shakes his head, tips the image of his mother from his mind and replaces it with Betty. Here are Betty's large brown areolae folded under at the bottom quarter. Here are her nipples, flat now and just lightly flushed. But not for long. In Harry's mind he licks them intently as if he's removing cream from the bottom of a bowl, they harden and spring forwards to meet his tongue. That's enough now. They're hard enough to suck. He lets his trousers fall around his ankles. Things are well distended down below. One hand tugs his cock, the other reaches out into the night for balance. It occurs to him that Betty's house is behind him – that his naked rump is pointing towards her. It doesn't seem right – it seems impolite somehow. He shuffles around until he's facing in her direction. And he's grateful that her lights are out when he spills across the grass.

Harry's mind's-eye picture of Betty's breast is her actual breast. The first summer she moved in next door Harry strolled over with a bucket of loquats to say hello. It was early, just after milking. Betty was sitting with her baby on the verandah. There were boxes behind her in various stages of unpacking and a tea chest overflowing with balled-up newspaper. White cabbage moths hung on the tips of the long grass of the front lawn. Betty's face rosy with sleep, one soft breast exposed to the morning air, her bare feet dangling square and sturdy beneath her ... He looked for less than a minute, just long enough to set the detail of the scene in his mind – the glorious jugged curve of the breast, a hint of wetness at the nipple, the small closed face of the baby – then he stumbled over Michael's scooter lying partly buried in the grass. Betty looked up. He noticed her hair moved oddly around her face – in a stiff mass, like it was matted from the pillow. She looked startled. Her mouth opened and he thought she might scream. He dropped the bucket and ran.

If a cow is empty after two attempts at bulling (or artificial insemination) the best place for her is the butcher. A cow is full for two hundred and eighty-three days before she has her calf.

The udder of the cow is made up of four glands or sections, each with its own outlet or teat. The orifice of each teat is controlled by the purse-string muscle. How the cow controls this muscle determines if she is a hard or an easy milker.

If a cow aborts, due to contagion, the calf and membranes should be burned, buried where they lie, and a fire lit over the whole area. Unslaked lime should be spread over the charred calf before the hole is filled in. The cow is now a carrier. On aborting she will have licked her mucus-stained hindquarters and then her shoulders and sides. Other cows will lick these areas. The whole herd is now infected. Expect heavy losses.

An easy milker in the flush of her first lactation may need milking at lunchtime. A drop of collodion applied to each teat will prevent leakage.

Mastitis: prevention is better than penitence – be vigilant, follow the gospel of hygiene.

Rumen inoculation: take a partially chewed cud from the mouth of each mature cow and place it in the mouth of each calf; when it is swallowed the calf will ingest the correct germs for rumen digestion.

The milker should be encouraged to consider his hands as an extension of the udder. The same scrupulous standard of cleanliness applies to both.

A quality milker demonstrates a calm authority. He milks the herd fast and dry. The atmosphere is of relaxed arousal.

Two huntsmen spiders prowl Harry's bedroom ceiling. They've been hanging around for weeks in their opposing corners like boxers waiting on the bell. Both of them are dark and plump, the size of bread-and-butter plates. When he wakes up one of the spiders is on his pillow. 'Frankly,' Harry says to it, 'this is going a bit too far.' Edna's favourite cup tips off the draining board and smashes in the sink, his bootlace snaps in his fingers as he is tying it. Leaving the house to go out to milk he traps his thumb in the fly-wire door.

But here comes Pauline; her pleated feet, her thriftiness, the bunched flesh behind her knees, her pudding chest, her liquid eyes. The shy way she has of dipping her head as she steps up into the shed each morning, as if she thinks she must push against the dimness to be let in. He reaches for her udder. The first milk spurts over the back of his hand and drips between his fingers. It's as warm as blood.

The first egg was laid on Sunday,
by Wednesday
there was another.
It takes only a few days to make an egg,
and comparatively it is much smaller,
and no doubt easier
to birth,
than a child.

*Mues assisted with the mirror stick.
He's not much chop at holding it still.
And looking through binoculars
is dangerous at height
– all of your weight seems held
in the eyes.
I nearly toppled off
the dairy roof.

September 10
4.50 am – just after dawn.
A few stars still linger as I climb.
Mum is absent.
There are two white eggs
of roughly equal volume
on the floor of the hollow.

The eggs are warm and the air too,
her body heats the hollow
– makes a woody oven of it
so the eggs continue baking
even when she is away.
I don't pick them up,
just mark them with the crayon,
one, two,
and climb down quickly.
The day feels a bit special
and I keep thinking back on them,
the family clutch
– two pale moons baking in a tree.

Club-Toe is a poor incubator;
sloppy,
reluctant even.
She hops inside dutifully at the change of shift,
but once Mum or Dad
have flown away
she's off;
loafing,
preening,
falling into a mid-afternoon torpor
on some distant branch.

When the parents return
she darts back in again,
pretending
that she never left.

September 26
5.10 am
Mum leaves the nest
just as I climb.
There's a decent breeze;
the threat of rain later.
The noise of the wind in the leaves
sounds like washing on the line.
I suppose the egglings
can hear it all
– maybe a little muffled through the shell?
They are grubbier and moved in position,
all in good nick though.

Did you see the morse code lightning
when that storm came in last night?
I worried that the nest tree
would be struck,
and when Sip finally stopped howling
I fell asleep
and dreamed the eggs were in my bed.

October 7
I climbed mid-morning
with Dad on duty
– watching from a nearby tree.
Egg one is still largely intact.
Egg two has a large fracture
and I heard,
distinctly,
the tapping of the egg-tooth against the shell
and the imprisoned bird
croaking
as if requesting assistance
It is the first time
I have been addressed by an egg.

A lot of action today;
comings and goings.
On the ground, directly beneath the hollow,
a small rubble of shell.
Even considering some shell
may have been eaten,
or not ejected from the nest,
or carried off by another animal,
when I attempted a reconstruction
one egg

was all I got.
I think we can safely say
that egg two was never fertilised
and didn't hatch.

The tink tink of the bellbirds
is a constant backdrop
to the day.
The kookaburras assemble and call
as the sun slips from the trees.
Then there is quiet for a while.
It's only later
that an owl announces herself
out of the dark.

A change in the family is noted.
An added excitement and cohesion,
a lot of chorusing in wild bouts
throughout the day.
As if they are announcing to the district
this addition to the family
and congratulating each other
on the hatching.

I won't climb again
so as not to disturb the bub,

or risk a beak
in the back of my skull.

It seems plausible to consider
that birds were the architects for trees.
A hollow,
or a fork,
for every nesting cradle;
a branch for every grip.
And they designed a structure
to which insects are naturally attracted,
like women to the ohopo.

Twenty days it takes,
before the bub
appears at the lip of the nest.
Squat and glum
– a greasy piece of equipment,
more echidna than bird,
with its pin feathers sheathed in their quills.
Mum makes no attempt to clean the nest chamber.
It must be bedlam in there
after a month of shit
and leftovers.

Club-Toe is an atrocious feeder.
She drops her catch
just outside the nest,
or brings up a leaf or a twig.
When left in charge she deserts her post.
But sometimes I see her,
staring dolefully into the chamber,
nest-struck,
love-lorn,
jealous?

Dad caught a fence skink this afternoon,
a good six inches long.
He flew it home
stopping twice for a breather,
and perched on the edge of the nest
to feed it in.
Then he sat and watched
as every few minutes an inch or so
of skink
was hoicked up
into the nest.
I didn't get a good look at the bub,
but it must be a corker
to swallow such a meal.

Betty had a rabbit knitted out of grey wool. Her brother had a parrot, only he wasn't meant to have it, being a boy and being older, so the parrot had no name. The outside of the parrot was covered in green corduroy. Inside there was sawdust that smelled musty and damp when it rained and made them sneeze when they threw it around. Mostly they had the rabbit and the parrot in their beds, but if they went out playing a pretend picnic, a pretend family, or some sort of pretend sport, they took them with them. The rabbit was called Kit and Betty loved it.

Betty's mother had a long, sad face with wide-set eyes. Betty's father said, 'Mother, you have a face on you like a camel. Can't you smile, Mother?' Her teeth were bad from cough medicine so she tried not to smile and if she did smile she put her hand up so it looked instead like she'd had a shock.

There were curtains with marigolds on them and a hallstand for hats and umbrellas. The tips of the umbrellas sat in a metal cup. After it had been raining and a wet umbrella had been dripping Betty and her brother would take turns in drinking the tinny umbrella water from the cup. They were a year apart. He was older, but he was slow to talk and she was slow to walk which evened things up.

The father sold curtains in a department store in Melbourne and walked to work or, if it was threatening rain, caught the tram. He didn't have a briefcase; he had a newspaper folded long and slim in his hand like a bat. Sometimes he brought material home folded up inside the newspaper. He unwrapped the newspaper on the kitchen table and showed Betty how it had been folded just perfectly so it came to the edges, but not enough so as to stick out. The material was smooth again as soon as he unfolded it, no wrinkles. There was a green and blue check which became her new pinafore and more of the marigolds for cushion covers. When Betty saw a man on the street with a fat newspaper she tried to guess what colour material he had in it and what it would be made into.

Betty was the bee's knees, the cat's meow. She sat on her father's lap when he got home from work and held the ashtray for him. On Sundays he did things around the house. Even Betty could see the way he held the hammer down near its ears was wrong. He told her brother to hold the nail while he hit it and then he hit it hard so the top of the nail – the hat of it – pushed right through the skin of the boy's finger and gripped it tight against the wood. The boy screamed and the mother came with a cloth for the blood. The father said, 'What's all the fuss about?' He smiled at Betty. The deep lines on either side of his mouth looked like cuts.

Betty and her brother stood on the step in the morning to say goodbye to him before they got ready for school. The boy never said goodbye so Betty said it lots of times in different sorts of ways to cover up. As the father went through the gate he looked back at them and he said, 'Buy! Buy!' because he was going to work selling curtains and it was a joke.

The lady next door went away and they had to feed and water an old carthorse she kept in a paddock across the road. The horse belonged to her dead husband so she didn't like to get rid of it. The horse had patches of white fur on its back where harness sores had been and yellow teeth permanently on show between its floppy lips. When they put the hay in the hay net the horse didn't walk towards it or even blink at them, but the hay was gone the next day. They called the horse 'The Husband'.

The father told them they should clean out the paddock. One corner, where the horse stood, was platformed with layers of hardened manure. It was impossible to break through the manure and they didn't want to get too close to the horse.

Instead they trawled around near the fence collecting pieces of broken glass. They had a small pile of green glass when an older boy rode past on a bicycle. He rang his bell at them, it was shrill and jangly. The sun went behind a cloud. Betty's brother was suddenly frightened. He said they had to get rid of the glass. He started to pick it up and throw it into the old bath the horse drank from. Betty came and helped him. The glass floated for a few seconds on top of the water and then sank. It seemed mysterious, sacred, watching the glass sink. It felt to Betty like a kind of return. Betty said, 'Water to water, rust to rust,' like she had heard in church, then they put hay in the hay net and filled the bath up with water. The rabbit and the parrot had been watching them from the gate. They collected the rabbit and the parrot and went home.

The father's shirtsleeves were rolled up, but he still had his hat on. He hadn't put his hat on the hallstand yet and Betty thought that meant it was safe. One of his sleeves was wet. The line between the wet material and the dry material wasn't sharp like Betty would have expected, it was blurry.

The father took the boy by the arm. He put his other hand in front of the boy's face. It was cupped full of the wet green glass.

'Did you do this?'

'No,' the boy said.

'Did you do this?'

'No,' the boy said and started to cry.

'Don't you dare lie to me.' The father threw the glass at the wall, then he unbuckled his belt. He pushed the boy towards the kitchen. He said, 'There are no liars in this house.'

Betty went to get the parrot, but it was too late.

Betty had a job in the food hall. She went to the cool room in the basement and collected the cheeses on a trolley that had PROPERTY OF THE CHEESE DEPARTMENT written on the side, and at the end of the day she wrapped the cheeses in white muslin cloths and put them away. The large cheeses sat on wooden boards and stuck to them and made sucking sounds like a tongue inside a wet mouth when they were prised free. The cheeses were heavy and when she was lifting them she thought they were as heavy as babies. All the young women were cutting their hair and taking up smoking and leaving their long skirts behind. They stood and smoked under the shop awnings before work in the morning. They leaned their smooth heads together and puckered their lips as they lit each other's cigarettes. Betty had a green felt hat the shape of a melon with an egret feather on the side and no brim. The hats suited the women who had long necks; they looked like tulips. Women with short necks and square shoulders looked like they were wearing a bucket.

Michael's father liked soft cheeses that had to be cut with a wire. The first time he waited for her after work and saw her without her hairnet on, he said, 'Thank God for that.' They went to the pictures and ate spaghetti sitting on high stools at a bar on Bourke Street. They walked through the Fitzroy Gardens in the dark, the possums scattering away from their footfalls. He settled her at the base of a giant fig tree and removed her bra and placed his head and hands inside her blouse. He kneaded her breasts between his fingers, then rubbed his face against them, leaving the mark of his stubble against her where the skin was paper thin, almost transparent, where the blue veins twisted through the flesh towards the nipple like strings of ivy. She looked down at the dark silhouette of his face between her breasts. She heard his lips ping as they parted, as he opened his mouth and reached out for her nipple with the pointed tip of his tongue. He turned the nipple in his mouth, rolling it backwards and forwards. She whimpered. She looked up at the dark folds of the tree and then back again at his face. He wasn't so young. The skin around his eyes was crisscrossed with lines; she traced them with her fingertips. She wondered how people resisted. How was it possible to resist?

He held her hand on the tram, behind her handbag. She stroked his fingers. She found herself telling him about a puppy her father had brought home for her tenth birthday: a black spaniel. The puppy didn't grow and had to be coaxed, stiff and costive, out of its kennel in the morning. When she gave the dog its first bath in the copper the water pooled around his neck. Running her hand over the humid curls she had felt the tufted fur where a collar had been. They made another collar for the dog – out of a cut-down belt – and Betty remembered being relieved when the worn-down place on the dog's neck was covered again. She swallowed to show that the story was finished. The man nodded and drew his lips back in a smile; he had nothing to say about this.

It wasn't the story Betty had meant to tell the man; she meant to tell him the funny thing about the dog – that when it was asleep it would start growling under its breath, then barking and then, while still fully asleep, it would jump up and run head first into the nearest wall and wake up shocked and affronted that they were laughing at it.

Later, in her bed, Betty remembered the man's hands on her. She remembered stroking his fingers on the tram and she knew why she'd told him the story about the black spaniel. A long-worn ring leaves the same braided indent on the skin after it has been removed as a collar. The mark isn't visible to the eye, but it gives itself up to touch.

When he was gone and she was pregnant with Michael and made the first of her moves away, she forgot exactly how it had felt; the unstoppable desire. Later still, when she was working nights in the hospital laundry at Bendigo and watching Michael play on his own, she was the one who took control. Every Tuesday and Thursday night for a month she made a bed on the floor of the storeroom and lay with the nightwatchman there. The humid smell of bleach rose from the clean sheets and from his spill, white too and milky like an expensive cleaning fluid. Bolder now, she drank it, she smeared it over her breasts, she felt it sticky between her thighs as she bicycled home from work. And stripping for her bath she noticed how it formed a coating as it dried and could be peeled like sunburn – like it was already becoming a type of skin.

When Little Hazel was born Betty told Michael that his new baby sister had a present for him. She gave Michael the green corduroy parrot. The grey rabbit, her rabbit, she gave to Little Hazel.

*'A neatly patterned yoke adds charm to this simple jumper for your small daughter.'*

The *Victorian Dairy Farmer* brings them together. The weekly broadsheet is aimed at the dairy-farming family. After Harry has read about butterfat production in New Zealand and the threat of margarine he tears the family pages out with a ruler and takes them next door. Betty reads the short stories, the articles on nutrition by 'calorie', the reports from the wives of dairy experts accompanying their husbands on technical visits to Berne or Reykjavik or Idaho. She also reads the back of the farming page so she can engage Harry on dairy topics.

'Do we have that weed St John's Wort around here, Harry? It says in the *VDF* a German woman with a yen for gardening brought it to Victoria and it escaped at Bright racecourse. It causes hyper-mania, depression and skin problems in cows. How on earth does a plant escape at a racecourse?'

When Betty raises the problem of 'pugging' in dairy pastures she finds Harry keen to explain and then to explain further … Betty thinks Harry talks about his pasture the way some women talk about their hair. The pasture, like a woman's hair, is always under some program of improvement or repair. There is generally a difficult stage it has to go through and myriad problems in regard to low yield or poor establishment along the way. Inundation with water can wreak havoc. When things are badly poached a light harrowing is required. Betty keeps her thoughts to herself until he mentions the need for a roller. She looks up at him from her crochet. 'I've heard a heated roller is good, Harry. What about using a heated roller on your poor grass?'

Harry is struck by how much simpler things seem when they are written about in the *VDF* than in actual life. The dangerous job of hoof trimming, for instance. *'Trim the hoof to distribute the weight evenly between the two claws of the foot, leaving sufficient horn to protect the corium or inner hoof, then trim the claws to their normal size and shape.'*

Some years back he was so taken with an article on an organic manure spreader he went ahead and ordered one. Harry has the standard machinery – a mouldboard plough, a cultivator of the rigid-tyne type, a middle buster, a bedder and an automatic-tying pick-up hay baler. All of this pulled by a dark red twelve-horsepower Massey Ferguson that Little Hazel calls 'the tomato'. According to the *VDF* organic manure spreaders were all the rage in the USA. Manure from the cowshed is loaded into the liquid-proof hopper which is towed into the paddocks by tractor. The mechanical spreader at the back of the implement works the ground and scatters the organic material (cow shit) evenly. There's a step missing, of course: the cows don't shit directly into the hopper – Harry has to shovel it. Around fifty shovel loads of dripping, liquid shit per milking. 'Fucking Americans,' Harry chants under his breath as he pours more and more fuel into the tomato and rides it across the paddocks spreading shit and stopping constantly to unclog the choked outlet shute. 'Fucking bastard Americans.'

Little Hazel reads 'Skipper's Mail Bag' every week and adds up the small sum awarded to the children who send in a poem, a joke, a drawing or a photograph to be published. She despises Myrtle Broad from Mologa who repeatedly sends photographs of herself on her white pony getting the Good Hands trophy at the local show, or a drawing she's done of a rearing horse that is so clearly copied out of a book you can see the tracing marks. Little Hazel knows she could do better. She never sends anything in, but this doesn't stop her looking for her own name in print as she reads and feeling disappointed when it isn't there. One school holidays she does write away – she replies to an article on pen pals through the American Australian Association in Nebraska. She requests an Indian girl or boy with a spotted horse, but nobody ever replies.

# HAZEL REYNOLDS'
## NATURE DIARY

*July*

*To-day one of the girls bought a goldfinch nest for the nature table. It had three broken eggs in it. A goldfinch is a pretty little bird that likes to flaunt the feathers of its wings.*

*To-day we saw a dead baby rat hanging in the fork of a bush. Our teacher said a butcher bird had probably left it there for later.*

*August*

*There are six nests in the trees near the bins. Five are in the trees. One is on top of the water tank cover.*

*To-day we wrote a bird list for our school and did a graph of it.*

*September*

*We found a baby mudlark on the ground behind the shelter sheds. It has been very windy and we think it was blown out of the nest. We can't see the mother. We brought it inside and our teacher put it in her desk drawer on the duster cloth. We aren't allowed to keep looking at it.*

The baby mudlark is still alive. We made a shoebox for it
to live in and the teacher feeds it sugar water with an eye
dropper. It can be very noisy when it is hungry.

To-day we had a competition and the baby mudlark is
called Smudgy. My name was Lord Feathers but it only got
one vote. Smudgy comes out of his box sometimes and sits
on a plate on the teachers desk. He squawks when we
go past.

Smudgy can stand up properly and walk a few steps but
he tips over a lot and falls on his beak. It is very hard to feed
Smudgy because our fingers are too big to go down his throat
We use a crochet hook with a fly on the end of it.


October

To-day we put Smudgy outside on the grass under a laundry
basket. Smudgy is trying to catch his own flies now. We saw
him with a grasshopper in his beak but it might have been
already a dead one.

To-day when Smudgy was outside we saw a butcher bird
flying nearby and the teacher went and brought him back
inside.

When he is in the classroom Smudgy likes to stay close to
Mrs Marmalade, the school cat.

November

The dentist is visiting and Smudgy likes the dental van.
He goes inside and pecks at the drills and mirrors. We had
to catch him and keep him inside when the dentist was
leaving.

To-day a new bird came to the bird table. We are not sure
what it was but we drew pictures of it. It was small and sang
with a silvery note.

To-day our teacher said she thinks Smudgy is a female
because she has white eyebrow feathers and white under her
beak. When we were cleaning out Smudgy's box we found
a lot of hard pellets with bits of wings and cricket legs. The
pellets were hidden under the straw.

To-day Smudgy flew from the teachers table to the library
corner. It wasn't very straight but she landed well. We all
clapped. She is very beautiful now.

A kind lady is minding Smudgy and Mrs Marmalade
over the long weekend. The lady collected Smudgy in a shoe
box. My special cousin who is an albino is coming to stay
with us.

When we came to school this morning our teacher told us
that our Smudgy had been killed. We don't think it was
Mrs Marmalade because she is always sleeping. The other

*thing I didn't say about Smudgy is that she liked our*
*teacher's earrings. Her favourite ones were the white ones.*
*They are made of plastic and shine when they catch*
*the sun.*

Shirley Timms wins the nature diary prize with a picture of
Smudgy made from uncooked rice. Hazel Reynolds comes
second. Harry leans against the gate and reads Little Hazel's
nature diary while she runs Foot Foot through her exercises.
With her black school shoes and white ankle socks Little
Hazel's feet look like another set of hooves skimming over
the cape weed. Both girl and heifer are breathing hard when
they return to the gate. Harry smiles at her and straightens the
collar of her school blouse. 'Well, you're a chip off the old
block,' he says.

Little Hazel gives Harry the nature diary to keep. In return
he buys her a pair of her very own binoculars – they are the
same as Michael's, but in a tan leather case.

Little Hazel checks on Foot Foot from her bedroom
window when she wakes in the morning and sometimes turns
the binoculars in the direction of Mues's place over the road.

Michael uses his binoculars to look down Dora's blouse
when they go out picking mushrooms together.

Betty sometimes borrows the children's binoculars and stands on the back step scanning the paddocks thereabouts.

Harry's binoculars hang from a brass hook in his kitchen. He uses them for birdwatching and checking the cows when they are in the back paddock. He makes his regular observations of the kookaburras and sometimes he finds they come in handy for checking next door – making sure Betty's car is in the garage and that her chimney is giving off smoke.

Harry takes Michael down the hall and stands him in front of the yellowing mirror.

'Relax your face; just let it go to putty. Jaw as well. Let your mouth hang open. Lovely. A very pretty picture. Now close, slowly, slowly.' Harry grips Michael under the chin, gently lifting his lower jaw back to meet the upper.

'There. Hold it just there.'

Michael looks in the mirror. There he is; sweaty fringe sticking up on his forehead, a dusting of blackheads across his nose, one eye looming larger than the other. Harry's hairy hand cradles his jaw.

'Can you see it?'

'What?' Michael struggles to speak out of his squashed throat.

'There. The mouth. When the mouth is held like this; relaxed. The lips just closed together, not pressed or forced. They leave an exact shape, an exact triangular nub-like shape in the middle. Fit the tool to the job, boy; what shape is that?' Harry's thumb is pressing against Michael's windpipe.

'A circle?'

'Right. And not just any circle. A nipple. I think, Michael, that we are not all alike. I suspect that not all male mouths and female nipples go together. But somewhere, somewhere out there is the perfect fit. The mother's nipple is always a perfect shape for her child, of course. It's a great pity that we don't remember more about those early experiences at the breast. But what I'm saying is adult to adult, male to female, somewhere out there is a woman you could go to sleep with at night attached to her breast and both wake in perfect comfort. Nice thought that, eh?'

Michael shakes Harry's hand free.

'So what am I meant to do then – go to my mates' places and ask if I can put my lips around their sisters' nipples just in case she's the one?'

Harry takes a step backwards. He hadn't reckoned on questions or disagreement.

He takes his hat from the hallstand.

'No. I admit that, Michael. I admit that it mightn't be straightforward finding these things out.' He turns for the front door. Perhaps writing is better than demonstration? 'Back to the silage now.'

*Skin. The female is covered with two types of skin. The skin of the body is easily observed on the torso, arms, legs and face. It is essentially the same as the skin of the male, but cut from much finer-grained stuff. The sexual organ (I'm talking inside front of underpants here, Michael), breasts (esp. nipples) and lips feature a skin uniquely inflamed with blood. Unlike the ordinary body skin (and male skin), where the blood runs in controlled networks of veins and arteries and sub-veins and sub-arteries (think horticultural drip-and-pipe irrigation), the blood in the sexual areas is right at the very surface. Blood constantly replenishes itself to these super-sensitive sites and 'sprays' up to the surface causing redness and engorgement (consider the erective nature and structure of the nipple).*

*You'll be knocked out to discover that the skin of the inner folds of the sexual organ is not smooth, but rough! I'm not*

*talking a corrugated track here, more a beaded or pearlised*
*oatmeal, but it is indeed rough. This wasn't clear to me until*
*I'd made a number of investigations as it is hidden in the 'wet*
*female' by her secretions. The skin texture of this area can only*
*be accurately observed in the compliant 'dry female'. Poor*
*education of males on these subjects has many believing (and*
*expecting) that the female sex organ is simply a second pair of*
*lips spliced in sideways between the legs and opening onto the*
*front passage. The structure of the female sex organ is complex*
*(more on this to follow) but as for the skin, expect a wattled*
*texture (think poultry). The raised wattles or nodules burred into*
*the skin encourage the flow of secretions to one particular area*
*and I don't doubt they also encourage the movement of the male*
*hand in this direction too. But let's not get ahead of ourselves.*

*Further to our earlier chat about breasts … Unlike other*
*animal species I have considered, the human male clearly*
*takes pleasure from the breast of the female (an instrument*
*for suckling offspring) and, added to this, from what I can*
*gather this is met with a degree of agreeability on behalf of*
*the breast owner. I would not be surprised if some candid*
*female admitted to self-manipulation of her own breasts*
*for pleasure. Further to this, I would not be surprised at the*
*'innocent' mutual manipulation of breasts between females*

*who are flowering or even sexually mature. If you pick up*
*anything on this, Michael, let me know.*

Harry felt his first female nipple at the age of sixteen. It belonged to Mary Bird, mother of Noreen Bird now at the counter at the co-op. They were petting on the edge of the creek in the shade of a strip of old tea-trees overrun with ants. Mary sat with her knees pulled up to her chest; he was cross-legged next to her. He couldn't really get at her like this, with her all folded up on herself. He had one arm around her shoulders as they kissed and would, every now and then, exert a bit of pressure on her upper body to try and tip her backwards. The bottle of Colgate Dactylis he'd bought for her bulged in his pocket. She was a chewy kisser, well salivated. When she broke off a string of spittle hung for a second between their mouths. She stood up and put her hands on her hips. She looked huge standing above him, her blouse billowing out from the waistband of her skirt. He saw her legs in close-up, shaved below, but the knees covered in spiked yellow hairs. She frowned down at the place she'd been sitting and used her foot to sweep the twigs and leaves away, then she gathered her skirt between her legs and lay down beside him. 'It's your job to watch for bull ants – alright?' she said, and untucked her blouse. Harry kissed her again. He threaded his hand through her clothes until it rested on the skin of her belly. Her skin was saturated with a flat even heat. The word pelt came into his mind. A digestive movement burbled inside her and he pulled back in surprise. She retrieved his hand and moved it higher up. He felt himself stiffening, the blood running heavily into his cock, drawing it out like an anchor pulling though water. He started to move his thumb. Slowly he stroked and gathered in the flesh and delivered it back to his fingers. She lifted her hand to brush a fly away from her mouth and then returned it to her side. He stroked and smoothed. Mary started humming.

'Harry.'

'Yes?'

'If you're looking for a tit, it's higher up.'

Mary was a strawberry blonde with a frizzy bob, thick arms and legs, and a firm, strong torso. She wasn't a stick. Harry had been working at her ribcage – the inflation between waist and chest. He walked his fingers higher up her chest, pushing under her bra. The breast had a disappointing flatness, the tissue settled deeply against the chest in the way of a liquid seeking the lowest point. And it was so inert, so without the bouncy sway he found hypnotic when she walked, or ran. He spread his fingers and felt the ringed flesh of areola and then the first pebbling of nipple. She moaned a little. He cleared his throat. He was grinning now, and feeling immensely proud – even if the initial geography was askew. He traced the circle of areola with his index finger and dragged his thumb gently across the middle where it struck the growing nipple so naturally, as if it couldn't be avoided, again and again.

Dora follows Noreen Bird and Edie Plimeroll up the wooden steps to the hall. Noreen wears a yellow dress with a matching knitted shrug. She's walking in an exaggerated bouncy fashion which causes her corsage to fall off and slip through the steps into a puddle below. The purple flower topples softly into the dirty water. Noreen looks down between the steps at the puddle, then up at Edie, and shrieks, 'Edie, Edie, Edie.'

Edie Plimeroll picks her way down the steps and around to the side railing where she stands with her hands on her hips looking at the flower listing sideways in the water.

'Oh God, Nor. It's ruined. You'll have to go home.'

Noreen's standing beside her now. She nudges the flower

over to the edge of the puddle with her shoe, bends down and picks it up.

'Bugger that. Des is getting his tongue in tonight or I'll kill myself.'

She shakes the wet flower violently, like it is on fire, and pins it to the collar of her dress.

Edie and Noreen trot back up the steps again and Dora follows them through the door. The band is tuning up. There's a loud rush of sound and a strong smell of Brylcreem and 4711. Dora hands in her ticket and gets a tin mug of cordial in exchange. The hall has been jollied up with dolls cut out of newspaper. Down one side the dolls have skirts; down the other they have trousers. Under the dolls, lining each side of the hall, are a row of chairs: boys and girls. Dora sips her cordial and looks at the dresses. Spearmint green is popular, and violet and yellow. She counts three flat pancake hats in the style of Queen Elizabeth. Dora is wearing Betty's tweed suit with a silk scarf tied around the waist. The scarf is keeping things in place. Betty has warned Dora not to dance too vigorously or she'll leave the skirt behind. Michael should be with her. She only agreed to come because of Michael. While Betty was helping her to get ready some boys from the butter factory came and collected him in an old Plymouth sedan with the back doors missing.

Dora places her mug on a chair and pats her hair. Eunice from the post office comes and sits next to her and they smile at each other when the band strikes up properly and the dancing begins.

Errol Carton dances with Betty Whipp, Sissie MacAdam dances with Reg Lillee. Mrs Collins dances with her son Donny – against his will. Edie Plimeroll dances with Des Carton. Iris Glassop dances with Donny Collins. Noreen Bird dances with Wes Popp. Noreen Bird dances with Des Carton.

Michael comes in after three songs have gone by. He is with two older-looking boys Dora doesn't recognise. The three of them stand slouched against the boys' wall sharing carefully from the same mug – too carefully for cordial. Michael's shirt is big on him, the shoulder seams sit way down on his arms and the cuffs have been folded back. His tie – Harry's tie, Dora supposes – is navy silk. She likes the way he's slicked his hair back behind his ears so more of his face is on view and his good trousers are pleated – adding some bulk to his hips and thighs. Michael and his friends stand a bit apart from the others. They talk and drink and watch the dancing and sometimes point at a girl.

A song finishes, another is about to start, when one of the boys makes his way across the floor. He is a tall boy with curly hair and a long, slightly crooked mouth. He walks over to Mavis Fehring – the prettiest girl. She toys with her gloves and pretends to be looking in the other direction. The boy touches her on the shoulder and she stands up and smiles in a bored, tired way as if dancing with this boy is another chore such a popular girl as her will have to endure. Mavis follows the tall boy as he walks around the outside of the dance floor looking for a place for them to dance. He's a very tall boy – probably six foot – so Mavis is almost trotting behind him on the toes of her painted green sandals to keep up. He's taking a long time to find a place; Mavis has followed him now for one whole lap around the hall. The boy passes Michael and his other friend and grins at them. Mavis is still trotting behind him. The song is well underway. Some of the couples who are dancing have slowed down to watch as Mavis follows the boy. She's done three laps now behind him, she's starting to cut the corners and her mouth has fallen open with the effort. On the fourth lap, the song half over, Mavis takes her eyes off the boy's back. She looks giddily around the hall. When she reaches the girls' wall she grabs for her chair and throws herself onto it. The boy knows straight away that she's stopped following him. He slackens his pace and saunters back to his friends. Michael offers him the mug and he takes a swig. There is some confusion about what has just happened. Mrs Collins bustles up and bends over Mavis sympathetically, but Mavis shakes her head and motions her away. Mavis sits for a while, then she stands and walks slowly and deliberately past the line of girls in the direction of the toilet. The colour on her shoes is lifting and she leaves a faint trail of green house paint in her wake. She doesn't come back.

For the next hour Michael's friends – the tall boy and the other boy, who has snow-white hair and pimples around his neck – ask several of the girls to dance. Sometimes they actually dance. Tall dances with Noreen Bird, Snow dances with Mary Carton and Sissy MacAdam, but other times they make the girl follow them around and around and around the dance floor, without ever turning towards her and opening their arms. After Mavis the girls are wary, but none of them refuse the offer to dance. They follow less doggedly though. Most of the girls only follow for a lap before they sit down again. Except for freckly Eunice. Snow asks Eunice to dance and she follows him around the dance floor for eight laps, for the whole song, and when the music is over she hovers nearby in confusion as he rejoins his friends and they laugh loudly.

Dora watches. Nobody has asked her to dance. When Mavis left, Dora tried to catch Michael's eye to show him her disgust, but he looked away. Mrs Collins bangs a spoon against a tin mug to gather their attention and announce the last dance. The band launches into a wheezy rendition of 'Blue Skies'. There is a scramble now, boys coming across the floor towards the girls, elbowing each other to get in first. Michael is standing in front of Dora. He's bending over a little at the waist and has his hand out with the palm up. Dora is angry, but she wants to dance, too. She stands up. Michael turns to claim a space for them on the crowded floor, it's the last dance after all, and it will all be over soon. Dora looks at his back receding in front of her, but she is so angry she can't follow him. She's getting jostled on the sidelines. Michael has been sucked in by the crowd. He looks back over his shoulder for her. He calls her name.

Dora returns her tin mug to the ticket table near the door and leaves. She runs down the steps and into the road and turns towards the creek. The sound of her sandals slapping against the road is comforting. The music from the hall reaches her in bursts, thinned out by the air – one long elongated note loud then faint, loud then faint. An owl hoots from one of the red gums. Michael catches her up on the bridge. She walks faster as he gets close. He follows her past the water tower, past the picnic ground, past some of the neater town houses with their flower beds and garden paths. It's darker on the outskirts of town. They leave the footpath and walk on the rough shoulder of the road. Michael puts in an extra step and catches up to her. He reaches out for the scarf around her waist and hooks his hand through it.

'Will you stop now?'

Dora keeps walking, pulling Michael along with her.

'You'll rip your mum's scarf.'

'Stop trying to get away then.'

He drags her back to him. He pulls at the thick material of the suit, feeling her stomach and her back and forcing his hands through the waistband of her skirt. His mouth is on her temple. He kisses her, almost on the eye, and says, 'I'm sorry, Dor. I'm sorry.'

She can feel the tendons working in his hands as he grabs at her belly and buttocks. She arches her back and moves his hands up to her breasts. She moans and unbuttons her blouse, pushing his head down to her nipples. They stumble away from the road into a stand of sugar gums that back on to Mues's place. Michael strips a few branches and makes a rough bed of leaves. She lets him remove his mother's jacket and untie the scarf around her waist. They find an elbowed branch to use as a coathanger. At the moment when she opens her legs and curls her hips up to meet the jab of his cock she turns her head and looks at Betty's empty suit hanging overhead. The material is soaked in moonlight – the buttons throw off chipped beams of light.

So this is how you do it, Dora thinks. You do it by imagining you are somebody else.

Slashing gorse in the shelterbelt Harry finds the nest of a striped honeyeater underneath the trees. It's a lovely article – a deep hairy cup of woven grasses bound with spider web and beak spittle. The outside of the nest is patterned; tawny and pale like the bird herself. Harry eases the nest into his pocket and forgets about it until later, until teatime when he's slicing his sausages and smearing them with chutney. He coaxes the nest from his trousers and places it on the table next to his plate; watching, as he chews, the suppleness of it as the flattened grass stems unfurl, little by little, to form the circular lip of the cup again. The expansion completed, the nest rolls softly onto its side and touches the back of Harry's hand. 'Whoa there,' he says to it, and his throat catches tight. As he rights the nest and wedges it between the salt and pepper shakers he realises that he knows too much. When you look at things for long enough they reveal themselves to you, and then they reveal some more. Harry with his four sausages; 'One for each limb,' his mother used to say. Harry at the kitchen table with his empty nest.

*I'm going to share this with you, Michael. I can't make it out myself, but it happened and it might be useful and that's that. When I was twelve years of age Mum took me along to a wedding breakfast for an aunty from Bendigo. We went down on the train. I was all gingered up in a cut-down suit of Dad's (away for the hay cutting). The wedding was a big fancy do. Mum had a new dress – peach lace. You'd think it was olden days because it went to the ground. There was something very sombre and mysterious about the shape of her in that dress. The breakfast was in an orchard at Eaglehawk. (Ate my first sugared almond and a peppery sausage brought in from somewhere foreign – Italy? Greece? Queensland?) Mum had a glass of sherry.*

*When the speeches were done Mum got up from her chair and wandered off a little way between the trees. She waved over to me and we went for a stroll together. All good enough fun.*

When we were a bit of a distance away she stopped and took up a stooped stance and cocked her head to one side. I was still holding her arm. I thought she was listening to something in the distance. Then I heard a distinct gushing sound. She smiled at me shyly and when we walked on I noticed a small puddle on the grass and the distinct smell of urine. Nothing was said. We just kept walking. I didn't know what to think. (But I'll admit that afterwards I thought about it a great deal.) Mum had always been very private in her doings before this. 'Facilities' were available not far away had she wanted to use them, and even if she had fixed on using the orchard it would have been easy for her to send me away on some errand or another. I got the feeling that she wanted me to know what she had done and, more than that, she wanted me to enjoy it and know she had enjoyed it too. I deduce from this that the female act of passing water might be pleasurable – that, similar to the male organ, the location of the urinary equipment has proximity to the sexual equipment. It occurs to me that the female passing water when standing (rather than in the seated or crouching position we are familiar with) might also experience a stronger stream (gravity) and therefore increased pleasure. Don't be fey about the female water, Michael.

On one (morning) coupling with Edna (first year of marriage)

*I noticed a fair wash of liquid over my thighs and member. My first thoughts were of an extra-copious ejaculation, but by the smell of the sheets later in the week I deduced that her bladder must have been engaged. It wasn't unpleasant, Michael. My memory is that it wasn't unpleasant at all. I've also read (but I can't for the life of me think where) about a fellow training to be a doctor. He had to assist at many births in the course of his studies and while down the business end of things he was often showered with great streams of urine – usually across the face – and he found it in no way distasteful.*

*Don't go too easy with touch, Michael. Skin thickness will be different in different women. (Some udders are upholstered in canvas, others in tissue paper.) The nodes and receptors that sense touch are buried in the skin. They are a mixed lot – some nodes are in the outer layers, some are right on the top. You're aiming to touch her firm and sharp. The touch that elicits the strongest pleasurable feeling is just a few calibrations short of the touch that produces pain. And cut your toenails, Michael. When you are prostrate touch isn't just about the hands. A foot can be used to stroke the lower limbs of the female. (Asiatics consider the female foot an alternative sexual organ.) I once took a fair-sized piece of skin off Edna's shin with a hangnail*

*and she went off the boil for weeks. Your mother will have a*
*fancy file in her purse. Amery rub or board?*

*The male and female kissing equipment – mouth, tongue,*
*mechanisms of salivation – are strikingly similar, excepting*
*scale. Don't be influenced by the motion pictures. The kiss is*
*not a romantic condiment, but the first and essential course*
*of the full sexual act. In mechanical terms there are two locks*
*between the male and female: the genital lock and the oral*
*lock. The oral lock – the male placing his firm and extended*
*tongue into the mouth of the female where it prods and scrapes*
*her soft, bowl-like receiving palate, gums and surprisingly*
*muscular tongue – serves as a foreshadowing for the female*
*brain, increasing lubrication in preparation of the genital lock.*
*    It might seem I've underdone this. But I'm confident of*
*a fair degree of natural canniness on kissing. The baby at*
*suckle on its mother's breast – the erect and dripping nipple*
*providing an early model for the tongue – creates a brain and*
*mouth memory that can be called upon in sexual maturity, or*
*on cusp of same.*
*    Keep your lips, teeth, gums and tongue in good nick,*
*Michael. Not just for now, but for the future.*
*P.S. Lipsticks and pastes should be removed.*

On the pin board in Betty's kitchen:

One of Louie's whiskers glued onto a piece of paper. Underneath in Betty's handwriting it says: '*1 x cat's whisker for reattachment.*'

A postcard showing a line of kookaburras on a branch all looking in the same direction with the caption, WHO SAID SNAKE?

A drawing that Michael did of his mother at age three. It could be mistaken for a potato, except for the rays of hair or sunlight that branch out all around her being. The drawing is grubby now and has many pin holes in it.

Little Hazel's immunisation card.

A no-fail pikelet recipe.

A library card.

Betty doesn't say something is broken, she says it has 'come from together' and she likes in the first instance to try and fix it herself. The crack in the back step widens over time. Every now and then a lump of concrete breaks off and gets walked across the kitchen lino. At the first hint of rain regiments of ants march along the crack and up under the back door on sugar raids. Enough is enough. Betty mixes a batch of cement in the wheelbarrow. It's a dull Saturday afternoon; a milk-and-water sky. Her hair is tucked under a scarf; she's wearing her oldest apron, the blue with the yellow ric rac that's coming loose. She walks across to Harry's to borrow a trowel. A scruffy young kookaburra is dozing on the fencepost as she separates the wires and doesn't wake when they wobble back into place. Harry, too, has plainly been napping when he comes to the door. One side of his face is a rumpled pink and his hair is sticking up. They have a cup of tea together while waiting for the butter to soften against the kettle. Then he stands behind her at the kitchen table and teaches her to trowel.

'Use your whole arm,' he says. 'Not just your hand. It's a bit like swimming.'

He guides her hand over the bread. She watches the golden curve of it as she makes the figure of eight. His fingers are firm around her wrist; the longest hairs of his beard just touch her cheek.

'You're getting it,' he says.

She picks up another slice of bread. The butter is soft behind the knife, a little sweaty. Harry is shorter with just his socks on and stands with his feet wide apart as if the flatness of the floor is unfamiliar to him. His stomach is making creaking sounds like a cupboard door opening and closing. Betty concentrates on the butter – transferring the glow of it smoothly and evenly across the bread. She leans back a little to steady herself. The buckle of his belt presses into her hip. He smells of pipe smoke and Ammolene. She holds the slice up proudly.

'Yes,' he says. 'Lovely. Cement is heavier, but it's the same principle; steadiness and restraint.'

He steps back from her and clears his throat. He reaches into a drawer for a clean tea towel, wraps the bread and butter, and places it in the pocket of her apron.

'There you go,' he says. 'A new skill and a bit of supper for later: all in one.'

Harry can't sleep. He can't get comfortable. He rereads his *Woman and Home*s late into the night, but once the light is off his feet start to twitch; the sheets are tangled around his legs, the bed feels tilted at an angle. His fitful sleep is infected with women. Edna and Betty appear alongside Vera the little secretary. He wakes and reaches for his pencil and an old envelope, scratching out notes by the moonlight that slants in the window. He draws a rough sketch with arrows to Vera's points of interest: *'Breasts: small but steeply pointed towards the nipple. Fleshy field around nipple shaped with great delicacy. Nipple bud of small width, but highish when erect. Nipple colour: pink rose. Thighs: white, with some vein show-through. Bush sitting at slight recession to hips when standing. Bush thick, gingery, with tufting around upper thigh. Rope line of fine ginger hairs tracking from bellybutton down abdomen and joining with bush. Buttocks creamy and lightly dimpled.'* The envelope shakes in his hands. A few weeks ago it contained a letter from the Water Commission about his irrigation licence.

Harry gets up and pads around the kitchen. He opens drawers and cupboards, searching for something, but barely aware of what it is. He finds Edna's sewing box. When Harry was a boy his father locked him and his mother in the laundry when he went out in the evening. The laundry had no windows and a dirt floor. They made themselves comfortable enough – his mother in an old string hammock, Harry in the copper – but often he couldn't sleep and would whimper in the dark. His mother tipped six sewing pins into his palm and showed him how to toss them lightly onto the dirt and then feel for them with his fingertips and pick them up again. Hours would go by with Harry throwing out the pins and picking them up again. He had to concentrate and be gentle; he had to count in his mind to make sure all of the pins were back in his hand before he tipped them out again. Edna's pins are in a Dr Scholl's foot treatment tin. Harry counts out six – surprised at how small and light they are in his hands. He gets into bed again with one arm dangling near the floor. He shakes the pins lightly in his hand like he is throwing dice, tosses them on the floor and starts to feel for them with his fingertips. Eventually he falls asleep. Half of the pins are in his hand, half on the floor – one has gently pierced the waxy outer skin of his thumb. It stands erect, a silver spine quivering in the dark.

The pierced skin on Harry's fingers is still rough in the morning. He can feel it as he stands at the trough washing his hands before milking. Any breaks in the skin are dangerous. There's a risk of infection and of transferring it through the herd. The cows call out wetly behind him, impatient at the delay. Pineapple is first at the gate. When he lets her into the bail she blows a wad of spittle out of her nostrils. One of her teats is already dripping. Babs pushes in next. The morning is upon him.

Later, Harry walks through the bottom paddock with an envelope in his hand for Michael. Always the worry over the bottom paddock. How to control the prickly pear? How to tackle winter bogs and the summer scalds? Harry aims to keep his head up when he walks through the paddock to Betty's, but it rarely works. He finds himself stopping and noticing how the prickly pear has extended its range, how hard and pale the soil is, how without give. Soil, he knows, is not a substance in and of itself; it is a layer, a transitional space. The farmer needs to keep his soil soft and friable, in a constant state of openness. Harry makes plans for the bottom paddock. He's considered ambercane, mangolds and possibly swedes. Root crops provide high yields of fodder of a relatively low food value, but they are good appetisers and good keepers. He's considered more exotic fodder crops, Japanese millet or Sudan grass: bigger rewards and bigger risks, too, with their build-ups of prussic acid. But he can't quite bring himself to act on these plans. The prickly pear has taken hold. It is encroaching on the path his boots have cut through constant traffic. Perhaps it's time to get the tractor out, he thinks. Perhaps it's time to clear this mess away.

I spent a good part of Sunday
with the binoculars
watching the bub coming
back
and
forth
to the rim of the nest
– looking out at the world,
with an attitude of thought,
and then retreating.

Bub
spent hours today
testing his bolero wings;
unfurling them
and looking out across their tiny span
as if checking twin umbrellas
for weather-worthiness.

There's a month still before fledging.
Bub jumps the cradle
just as the family goes on the moult
and are markedly out of sorts.
The pretty pup
(think two woolly pompoms, tacked together)
is parked in a thicket of low acacias

in case he falls
and he does
regularly fall.
For no particular reason
he unbalances
and tips off the branch,
tumbling over and over in the air,
barely stretching his wings
before hitting the ground.
His cries gather the family
in the branches all about.
They demand he get back in the air again.
Sometimes
one of them
will fly down
and beak-whip him around the head
for encouragement.
I'm thinking of building him an airstrip.
Just a cleared bit of dirt
for take-offs and landings
so we don't,
all of us,
have to put up with his crying
and the fear he'll be grounded
for good.

If a kookaburra damages
or loses
a feather
in mid-winter,
or even at the start of spring,
it must wait for this one annual moult
to repair
or replenish it.
Several weeks are spent
torpid,
dull-eyed,
introspective,
waiting gloomily
for the new feathers to form.

The owl lands on the guttering
above my bedroom window.
The sound of the tin under her claws
wakes me up.
An infant kookaburra is easy prey
so I'm awake
for a while,
worrying,
in the dark.

You wouldn't say they were good parents,
or good siblings,
nevertheless,
they keep the bub alive.
They tolerate his whining,
his feeble attempts to fly
and hunt.
And as soon as there is danger
they are fierce to protect and defend.
Instinct,
from where I stand,
from on the ground,
looks like love.

The latest on the family diet:
worms,
snails (they crack the shells against the anvil
outside the dairy),
rats,
mice,
yabbies,
skinks,
moths,
millipedes,

dragonflies,
spiders,
lizards,
cicadas,
eels,
frogs,
hatchling birds,
fish,
snakes,
dog biscuits,
sandwiches,
chicken drumsticks,
sausages prepared as picnic food,
and other dainties.

Mum has a large mood on her
when she's on the moult.
Breeding must be exhausting,
then there's a whole new kit of feathers
to grow
year after year.
She's the only bird
in the family
who gives her all.

They run in their new feathers
with flights around the boundary,
with trapezes
between the peppercorn and the creek trees.
Dad does the stick
– testing his new coiffure from above?
In the afternoon
the ladies hunt for frogs.

Laughing lessons
are provided for the bub.
His first attempts are chirpy;
fractured.
It's a good few months
before he contributes
with the maniacal intensity
of the others.
What sounds insane to us
is probably just their daily newspaper –
weather forecast,
births deaths and marriages,
bragging sports reports,
general news.

Bub is losing the muddy look about the head.
His top-knot is coming in white,
his eye-stripe dark and sharp.
The rubbery
black
baby's-beak
is maturing into bone.
He hardly begs
unless he sees the others with something tasty
and then it is only a reflex
that he's able to override,
and get back quickly
to hunting for himself.

For the first time
I see the son
feed his mother.
He brings her a beetle
and landing inaccurately on the branch
walks sideways
claw-to-claw
in shy delivery,
in his opening act
of bird desire.

By coming early on a Sunday Harry can watch her ironing in the kitchen before tea. It's dance hour on the wireless. The doors to the hall and the front room are open so the sound carries through to the kitchen. The smell of roast meat and scorched cotton: the pump and jiggle of her arms. She sways her head to the music, her cheeks are pink and her nose and chin are shiny. A bowl of water balances on the end of the ironing board; her stomach presses against the board, but the water doesn't spill. Every now and then she dips her fingertips into the bowl and flicks them over the cloth. Sometimes she forgets that Harry is watching and she allows her free hand to float up next to her and move from side to side – as if she is smoothing out the notes as they waft up to meet her on the moist, beefy air.

For his birthday Harry gets a birdwatching book from Betty, a poem about insects written by Little Hazel and a handwritten docket for three days' manure spreading from Michael. There's a roast dinner where Betty's potatoes are, they agree, the best of her lifetime. 'Enjoy them,' she says, basking wryly in her achievement. 'It's all downhill from here.'

When Harry gets home he places Michael's docket and Little Hazel's poem in the biscuit tin under his bed. His wedding ring is in there, with some sewing pins and a photograph of his mother. The bird book is English. Kookaburras aren't mentioned and it has a grating tone – as if birds exist for the sole purpose of providing gentlemen of the educated classes with a diverting interest.

*Any birdwatcher will of course be interested in the question – how do birds recognise one another? Is it call, posture or colouration – or is it a mixture of these factors? Some American colleagues completed a recent experiment to try to answer this question on a pair of flickers – a kind of American woodpecker. Male flickers have a distinctive dark moustache. A pair of flickers was observed engaging in classic courtship behaviour. The female was caught and provided with a false moustache. When she was released the male approached her confidently from behind and began to mount her. A few seconds later she turned her head to the side and he saw her moustache. Immediately he disengaged and went into his full anti-male aggressive display. He pursued the disguised female for over two and a half hours, repeatedly attacking her and trying to force her out of the nesting area. The experiment proves that the moustache, i.e. colouration, has a very real significance in bird-to-bird recognition.*

Harry marks his place in the book and goes over to the mirror. The top of the dressing table is stamped with overlapping circles where Edna's teacups have scorched the veneer. Because he doesn't shave, weeks can go by without him seeing his reflection. He removes his glasses and covers his chin with his hand. He tries to imagine himself beardless, but with a neat, curving moustache. It's a younger look, a jauntier look, the look of a film star or a salesman. As he turns his head from side to side in the mirror he notices that the tide line of his beard has moved. While the hair on his head thins, his beard is thickening and encroaching, taking over new ground. Without even trying he is becoming a stranger to himself. He gets into bed and thinks about the flicker. Is she still flying around the woodlands of America wearing her tatty false moustache? The pillow kneaded and placed at just the right angle, he lets his head drop and finds himself speaking Betty's words aloud: 'It's all downhill from here. It's all downhill from here.'

Betty sits on the back step after work with a cup of tea and Louie stretched out beside her. There's the sound of dishes clinking in the kitchen and a magpie warbling lazily from the fence. Her watch says it's past seven. There are badges to sew onto Little Hazel's brownie dress, smalls to rinse, sandwiches to make, homework to check. She touches her thumb to a single wiry hair sprouting from her throat, bending it from side to side. What if she stood up now and just started walking? What if she walked across the paddock and climbed through the fence and walked right up to his door?

Mervyn Plimeroll drives the milk truck for Gannawarra, Cohuna, Wee-wee-rup and Leitchville. It's a seven-day-a-week job, but on Saturdays Mervyn's boy, Leslie, comes along for the ride. Mervyn drills Leslie through his times tables and if they make up a bit of time on the open road, they stop and fish for an hour on the Gunbower, always making sure that the tray of the truck is in the shade. Occasionally Mervyn lets ten-year-old Leslie drive, which he does standing up in order to reach the pedals.

This particular Saturday is grey and overcast. A storm is rolling in from the plains. It seems to be passing overhead at height. Only the very tops of the trees are swaying and the odd raindrops that spatter against the windscreen land softly, as if they have fallen from a great distance. The truck is running hot. It struggles up the driveway from Harry's and once they turn on to the made road again Mervyn notices the needle on the temperature gauge is in the red. He pulls over and switches off the ignition. Father and son look at each other then, as they register the sound of the motor fading and the whistle from the radiator taking its place. Mervyn gets out of the truck and starts to lift the bonnet. He tells Leslie to go into the house over there, motioning with his chin at Mues's place, to get some water.

The house isn't far away and Leslie trots off at somewhere between a walk and a run. He sticks to the road for as long as he can. The surface of it appears to be getting darker in front of him as the rain spots join together and blot out the dust. Leslie judges his task as important, but it isn't the first time it has happened and it isn't an actual emergency. The house he is walking towards is much like any other old farmhouse on the outskirts of town. A higher level of dilapidation is obvious out here. In town the houses have some evidence of paint and an attempt at a garden. If he could have chosen one of these houses, houses more likely to contain a woman with flour on her apron, he would have. He pushes the gate open and waits for a second behind it in case the sound alerts a dog. No dog appears. He picks his way up the path to the front door. There is an old cane chair on the verandah, next to it an upturned hub cap full of cigarette butts, hundreds of cigarette butts. It's not something his mother would allow, or at least not so close to the house. He knocks on the doorframe, but he doesn't wait long for an answer. He steps off the verandah and walks through the long grass and fruit trees along the side of the house hoping to find a bucket out the back, and a tap, hoping to carry out his task without having to speak to anyone.

It's around the back where things have come even more undone. There are five or six corrugated-iron sheds in different stages of decay and corrosion; a couple of them have lost their internal timbers to rot so the tin is askew, like giant sheets of paper. In between the sheds there are piles of engine parts, kerosene drums, broken farm machinery, tools, pieces of harness, chaff bags. An old piano sits partially cut up, an axe across the stained keys. There are more disturbingly personal items too: rotten rags, rusty cooking pans, brooms without bristles, fishing rods, clothes, women's shoes of an old style not even his grandmother wears, books, hairbrushes, empty food tins, family pictures still in their glass frames. All of it brown and covered with dirt and being splattered by the rain. Leslie wonders what might be left in the house, if the house itself is empty with all of its contents strewn here in between the sheds. Looking at it makes him feel tired. A raindrop hits his arm and he licks at the skin where it lands. He looks in a couple of the sheds – empty, but with a smell of mould and manure. He's aware that's he's taking too long, that he hasn't found the water yet and his father will be wondering where he's got to. The next shed along is in better repair. It's larger and has a door. His attention is caught by a pile of dried-out cicadas that have built up around the doorjamb. The common ones, the greengrocers, are good for fishing. The papery bodies of the cicadas have lost most of their colour in death, but Leslie kneels down and fingers through them. He's searching for some of the rarer types, a floury baker, or a yellow Monday. His father, Mervyn, is coming up behind him, so at the moment Leslie stands up and opens the shed door he's startled by the weight of his father's hand on his shoulder and he looks up into his face to see if he is angry. Later Mervyn will tell himself that he arrived at exactly the right moment. And he will tell the police that his son did not see what he saw in the shed because he was standing behind him when he opened the door. In truth they both stood for several seconds adjusting to the dim light inside the shed. They saw the sheep lying on its side in the straw, its legs hobbled with a pair of reins and Mues behind it on his knees with his overalls down, the shoulder straps splayed out behind him like his own set of ties he had broken free of. They both saw the blue nightie lying in the straw next to the sheep. The sheep lifted its head slightly in the direction of the sound they had made with the door. Mues didn't stop, he didn't look up. He said, 'Shut the door.' And they did.

Mervyn walked Leslie back to the truck in front of him with a handful of his shirt collar gripped in his fist so Leslie thought he was in trouble and in some way responsible for what he had seen. His father told him to stay put in the cab of the truck. Leslie was too frightened to ask where he was going, or even turn around, but he watched his father in the rear-vision mirror as he ran back down the road and turned into the driveway of the dairy farm they had just collected from. Some time later he heard a motorcycle and saw his father riding behind the farmer who was also balancing a bucket on the handlebars. Rain was falling heavily now, but the two men stood behind the truck talking and made no attempt to stop themselves getting wet. A police car arrived. The policeman got out and talked to Leslie's father and the farmer then he put his hat on and walked towards the house. The farmer filled up the radiator of the truck from the bucket, got back on his motorcycle and rode away. Then his father climbed into the cab and started the ignition. Leslie didn't look at his father as they sat listening for the motor to catch; they both looked at the rain on the window in front of them. Then they drove away.

By the time the constable arrived at the house Mues had washed and dressed and was sitting at his kitchen table with a bottle of beer. The constable searched the outhouses and found an elderly sheep in the hayshed. A blue ladies' nightie was hanging from a nail on the shed wall. A drenching tube and a half empty bottle of Chinese brandy were found nearby.

Mues was charged with administering a stupefying drug with attempt to ravish, and committing an unnatural offence. The first charge was dropped before the hearing on the basis it was unlikely to succeed. It was considered unlikely a sheep could be further stupefied from its natural state, and the bottle of Chinese brandy was unavailable for chemical testing as it had disappeared from the police evidence cupboard. It was noted in court that Mues had kept the sheep for over ten years and it had been a full six-toother before relations commenced. Mues claimed he had not engaged in the act with any other of his sheep and he had no history of acting suspiciously with other animals in the vicinity. It was noted that he had never married or established a proper relationship with a woman and it was considered unlikely that any local woman would have him. In his defence Mues said, 'It was a ewe. It's not as if I'm a fucking homo.' He was ordered to pay twelve pounds into the court poor box. A destruction order was raised for the sheep.

Sunday evening. It's cold. Betty picks her way down the path to the outhouse. She can smell Louie's urine on the base of the lemon tree – ammonia and citrus. A few steps' detour to the chopping block and balanced there she can see across the paddocks to the outline of Harry's house. His curtains are open. The front window is a white rectangle – an ice cube of light. He's reading, probably, or writing, or listening to the wireless. There's nothing much to see. She gets down and continues up the path to the outhouse, leaving the door open to the darkness as she pisses. Her legs are bare under the hitched-up skirt and she looks down at her thighs, appraising them; considering their effect on another. An envelope wedged between the weatherboards catches her eye. She tilts it from side to side to read the front. It's addressed to Michael. The handwriting isn't young – a careful copperplate – it looks like Harry's. She thinks she might tease him about it. 'Harry,' she could say, 'Harry, you have lovely hooks and hangers.' She puts the envelope in her pocket. On the way back to the house she dawdles, her arms hugging her cardigan across her breasts. Without much thought she returns to the woodpile and mounts the chopping block again. She's steadying herself on the rough surface, worrying about splinters in her slippers, when the light from Harry's house snaps off. The window, the whole house, disappears instantly. She clutches her throat in surprise and blinks into the darkness. Cows are moving in the distance. She can hear the lazy stumble of hoof against dirt and can just make out their massed shapes floating behind the fence. The herd is heading for the trees and for sleep. She realises the cows have been watching him, too.

Harry doesn't blame her for being angry. People can't help but make associations. The difficulty is the two events coming together – Mues's trouble with the police and the discovery of his letters for Michael. One somehow makes the other worse. He understands when she closes the door against his explanations. It's the disgust around her mouth that turns his stomach. As he's walking away he hears the door open again behind him. He turns back smartly, his hands raised in a gesture of apology, of regret. Sip is pushed out of the narrow opening and the door is banged shut behind her.

Harry cries on the ground then. He doesn't even wait until he is on his side of the fence. It hardly seems to matter anymore; all of the old lines are broken.

If she'd asked him why he did it, he would have said because ignorance is cruel, and perhaps because it is what a father should do.

At thirteen Harry knew nothing. None of what he had seen in the paddocks and the bush seemed applicable to men and women – or at least not the buttoned-up and smoothed-down men and women of his acquaintance. One morning the teacher sends the older boys up to the vicar's house for a special talk. There are four boys. They walk up the hill to the manse kicking pine cones out from under the dark trees that line the driveway. The vicar doesn't dilly-dally after service; he's already home and back in his civvies. They are only admitted to the hallway, but they can hear a kettle steaming and the sound of the races on the wireless. The vicar stands in the doorway to the kitchen and thrusts his hands into the pockets of his trousers. He clears his throat and smiles vaguely at the pattern on the hall rug.

'It's common to have a build-up. Best thing is to rub the stuff out of the erect organ. You can do it for yourself. Your wife can most likely assist. The cleaning lady helps out here if the wife's away at her mother's. Make it regular or you're likely to go off your head for a bit.' The kettle starts to whistle. The vicar turns towards the kitchen and then looks back over his shoulder at Harry. 'Close the door behind you, lad.'

And that's what Harry remembers. He's thirty-three, for Christ's sake. It's his wedding night. He's thirty-three and unbuttoning Edna's blouse, fiddling with the awkward canvas harness of her bra, his cock buckled painfully in his underpants. The pressure on the tip of it is almost unbearable. And in his head over and over again, 'Close the door behind you, close the door behind you,' and the nasal drone of a maiden stakes at Moonee Valley as they come around the turn.

Harry dreams he is conducting surgery on himself. He's cut himself open with one incision from neck to groin and peeled back the twin flaps of skin and meat. The triangular bones of his pelvis are now exposed. They are chalky and dry and unconnected to any of the surrounding muscle and flesh. The pelvic bones have two wounds in them – circular with ragged edges – one on either side of the triangle. You would guess they had been made with a hand-held drill. Harry is aware of himself looking down at the wounds and thinking, 'Well that isn't good. That will need fixing.'

Betty will not speak to him. He has spent all afternoon under the mulberry tree on the front lawn at Acacia Court, taking a break only once to buy two bottles of beer and return with them to drink. He leans against the Waratah, one hand resting on the strip of Axminster glued to the tank, the other cooling around the beer. The net curtains are drawn across the long window in the front sitting room; they hang a foot or so short of the floor. A few dead flies lie behind the glass and further in he can see three pairs of slippers, the mottled flesh rising out of them like puddings. Every now and then Betty's white lace-ups appear among the slippers. She must be feeding the slippered men, helping them with their teeth, adjusting their dressing gowns. He resents this work she does, resents the people she cares for. Why doesn't she notice him? Why doesn't she come out to the lawn now and speak to him properly? Her tea break comes and goes. He finishes the beer, but keeps hold of the empty bottle. There are men in this town he has never seen without a beer bottle in one hand. He considers throwing the bottle into the hedge, but someone will have to pick it up. Betty bends down then, just once, in front of the window. The hem of her dress dips into view and he starts within himself as if the fabric is being drawn across his skin.

He rides out of town, past the cemetery and the butter factory; the saleyards are a mass of afternoon shadows as the sun picks out the posts and rails. He rides through weed blossom; gorse and ragwort flowers are sucked against his coat. The road follows the river for a few miles then peels away and curves across the Tragowel Plains. He opens the throttle. It's warmer out here – the plains have their own weather – the sun's eye opens wider across the flat. He moves up to third. He's doing thirty now – really moving – the ring and pop of the pistons has blurred into a throb. It's as close as you can get to cruising – except he's constantly checking the road ahead for potholes and getting up out of the saddle when the shakes set in. He slows down to second for the crossing at Mincha. Four white signposts mark the road in each direction: south to Pyramid Hill, west to Gladfield, east to Turrumberry, north, behind him, back to Cohuna. A stranger wouldn't know this place had a name – that a crossing of two roads surrounded by acres of flat paddocks was a place in itself. Harry helped his father cart hay at Mincha. Harry and his father and a dog in a dray with no springs summer after summer. Back at school the rhythm of the dray was caught inside him and he was always in trouble for rocking on his chair.

The road doglegs after Mincha, the land to the south is low-lying and inundated with brackish water, backwash from Kow Swamp. The beer is thick in his bladder and he pulls over to the side of the road to piss. Once the Waratah is warm it runs rich and doesn't idle easily, he has to sit adjusting the throttle for a few minutes until it settles. He moves away from the exhaust and pisses over the chipped gravel. A pair of brolgas stalk through the shallows in the boggy paddock to the south. He watches them strut along the waterline, their black rod legs hinging tentatively beneath them. The native companion. They must be able to see him standing up on the road and to hear the motorcycle, but they show no sign of it. The larger bird stabs at something in the mud then lifts its head. Harry can see the dark, hairy dewlap that hangs underneath its throat. A breeze lifts the feathers on the bend of the bird's neck and the pink, penile skin beneath it is exposed. The brolgas look ancient, foreign, misplaced somehow. He feels uncomfortable watching them, as if he is intruding.

He gets back on the Waratah and coaxes it through the gears. The road is deteriorating. He puts his hand out to block the sun from his eyes and feels the wind push back against it. He rides past a horse paddock where three sets of ears swivel at the sound of him approaching, and then receding, without lifting their heads from the pick. The hill is coming into view. From this angle it looks triangular, but nothing like the pictures of the pyramids he has seen in books. There is rubbish in the samphire on the roadsides – tufts of toilet paper from the daytrippers who come out to climb and picnic. His bowels feel full. It's either numbness from the ride, or the beer shits coming on. The hill blocks out the sun now and he gets a foretaste of the cold night air against his face. He rides carefully over the soft gravel in the car park and leaves the bike ticking and pinging behind him as he starts the climb up the path. His legs are weak, his neck aches from watching the road. He'd like to pack this in right now and be at home in his bed. The thing that's kept him going through the day has been imagining her eyes on him. When he waited on the lawn, when he rode out of town, when he stood up precariously on the pegs at speed and cornered too fast on the bad road, it was only possible because he had been able to hold the thought in his mind that she could see him. But he's too far away now and too much of the day has passed. He can't keep it up any longer. The cows will be waiting at home. He drops to his knees just a few lengths up the track and sits with his head in his hands. When it is finally dark and the day birds are silent he walks back down to the car park, kicks the Waratah into life and turns towards home. The headlamp picks up the road ahead of him, but not too far ahead, just far enough to see. And this turns out to be the best bit of the day. His thoughts are dulled; the night air is close around him. He watches the place on the road just ahead of the light, the dark place that is for a fraction of a second made light, and then curves away behind him.

Winter has arrived before its time.
I'm feeding silage a full month
early.
The family spends much of the day
torpid,
together,
on a branch.
No lizard lunches,
no snake suppers,
no stolen hatchlings,
fewer mice,
no grasshoppers.

Morning sunlight slices through the trees
catching the edges of their feathers,
their scruffy top-knots,
rousing them
for the working day.

Mum sings on her own this evening.
Her voice high,
unbodied.
Dad cocks his head to listen
as if he's waiting
to hear his name.

I put half a cold sausage in Sip's bowl
and went back into the kitchen.
Thirty seconds later
Sip lets off a heartbroken bark.
Club-Toe is pushing herself
off the edge of the verandah,
a fat cigar of sausage
in her beak.

Hunting is hampered
by the fog.
A whole morning can be wasted
waiting for the sun
to burn the mist away.
And if the afternoon is lean
a day goes by
without food.

Bub has not attended
evening chorus
or slept with the family
for four nights now.
I find him in an acacia by the channel,
clinging to a low branch as if readying himself
to fall.

He looks feeble;
close to starvation
in his first winter.

The lid from an old paint tin
serves as his plate.
Three holes drilled in its edges;
string to hitch it over a higher branch
and lower it
down to him.
A week of mince, molasses and raisins
for breakfast and for tea.
It's not possible
after all this time
to sit back
and just watch.

It would be a mistake to report
that the kookaburra family sings only
at dawn and dusk.
They chorus
when a chick first leaves the nest,
when a snake is captured,
when a defence post
or boundary needs announcing.

And there are other calls –
a gentle chuck
to locate each other during the day,
the nuptial squawk from Mum to Dad.
The family that sings together
sticks together.

The four of them
in the red gum behind the dairy.
They come at dusk,
one by one.
Mum, Dad,
Club-Toe
and Bub.
The remains of the family
assemble themselves
out of the greying sky.

Looking out of the kitchen window Betty sees a tea towel hanging stiff on the washing line. She lets herself out of the back door and walks towards it, the frozen grass cracking under her slippers. It is just after dawn and everything is close with fog. She squints up at the line. It is too small and shabby for a tea towel. The winking owl has died in the night gripping the line with its claws. The owl has swung below the line in the way of a trapeze artist. The white dish of its face glows, its baby's eyes are open, but covered with a granulated crust of ice. Betty shivers and rubs her hands on her thighs. She needs to pee. This winter has gone on too long. It's been too cold. Stan is dying now. Cliff is dead.

At work she thinks about the winking owl, the odd comfort of it on the line at night as she made her preparations for bed. She doesn't want Michael or Little Hazel to find it hanging when they get home from school, or Louie to pull it apart. She rings Harry on the office telephone to ask him to go across and cut it down. The telephone rings out three times before he answers and he's startled to hear her voice at the other end. She never rings, she always comes across. He's immediately anxious something has happened to one of the children.

There are some groceries to get after work and Michael's boots need collecting from the menders. The children have finished their chores when she gets in. Michael is lighting the boiler and Little Hazel has made a gymkhana for Louie out of books on the hallway floor. Louie won't jump, of course, and Betty can see from the twitch of her ears that it's been going on for some time. It's not until tea is over that Betty goes outside. The line is empty except for a few pegs. Behind it, over towards the back fence, there is a small mound of dirt. It has been patted down carefully. He's placed a line of stones there. Not in a rectangle, like they are marking a grave, but just loosely, following the slope of the ground.

Harry comes in the kitchen door with his belt undone. He takes Betty by the arm and leads her out to the hall. Then he gets behind her, nudging her along, his face is in her hair with its dank sweet smell. Hair washing is on Sunday. He pushes her forwards, the long bones of his thighs slap against her rump. She isn't protesting; she isn't pushing back against him, but it is more his will than hers. He boosts her through the bedroom door, shuts it quickly and pulls the curtains across the day.

Betty's breathing is shallow and fast. She reaches for the bedpost to steady herself. She can't look into his face now; not because she is wary of what she will see, but because her own face would be revealed in the looking. She holds her head to one side, just glancing at him as he shucks the buttons of his fly, pushes his underpants down and reaches for her. He plucks at her skirt, trying to find the edge of it, trying to get it out from between them. He tells her to turn around. He moves her legs apart. 'Likes this,' he says, pushing his hands against her thighs. She recognises the peculiar burr in his voice, but it is the sound of her skirt crushing between them as she turns that is, she thinks, impossible to resist. He puts his arms around her and undoes the buttons of her blouse. He lifts her breasts out and over the top of her slip. They both look down. Betty shudders at the sight of her nipples swaying before her. The taut material of the slip pushes her breasts upwards and together.

'Oh,' she says. Harry buckles forwards, leaning heavily against her. He has a breast in each hand. He squeezes, releases, feels the weight of the flesh between his fingers, runs his thumbs over the nubbly bud of each nipple. Some fumbling between her legs. He pushes her knickers aside, thrusts his cock between the lips of her sex. With his hand underneath he makes a sort of seal and slides into a rhythm of push and pull. Betty comes first, gushing and losing the strength in her legs so he is standing behind her holding the whole weight of her in his wet hand.

Another thrust and he says, 'Oh Jesus.'

Betty reaches behind him so she can feel the kick of it through his rump. They lie down on top of the counterpane. Harry on his back, Betty tucked under his armpit and folded half across him, her little racked belly spreading out across his hip. He stretches down and kisses the top of her head. 'Looks like rain tomorrow.'

*Mateship with Birds* is the title of a book of bird notes by Australian nature writer Alec Chisholm. It was first published in 1922 and can still be found in opportunity shops and second-hand bookstores. I recommend it highly.

Alec Chisholm was born in Maryborough, Victoria, in 1890. He left school at twelve and had a long and distinguished career as a naturalist and journalist. As a young man, Chish (as he was known to his mates) worked with the poet Mary Gilmore on a campaign to halt the slaughter of egrets for women's feather hats. He died in 1977.